THE PELICAN SHAKESPEARE

GENERAL EDITOR ALFRED HARBAGE

JULIUS CAESAR

WILLIAM SHAKESPEARE

JULIUS CAESAR

EDITED BY S. F. JOHNSON

PENGUIN BOOKS

PENGUIN BOOKS
Penguin Books Ltd, 27 Wrights Lane, London W8 5TZ
(Publishing & Editorial) and Harmondsworth,
Middlesex, England (Distribution & Warehouse)
Penguin Books, 40 West 23rd Street,
New York, New York 10010, U.S.A.
Penguin Books Australia Ltd, Ringwood,
Victoria, Australia
Penguin Books Canada Limited, 2801 John Street,
Markham, Ontario, Canada L3R 1B4
Penguin Books (N.Z.) Ltd, 182–190 Wairau Road,
Auckland 10, New Zealand

First published in *The Pelican Shakespeare* 1960
This revised edition first published 1971
Reprinted 1973, 1974, 1976, 1977, 1978, 1979, 1980,
1981, 1983 (twice), 1986 (twice), 1987

Library of Congress catalog card number: 73-98369

Printed in the United States of America by
Kingsport Press, Inc., Kingsport, Tennessee
Set in Monotype Ehrhardt

CONTENTS

PUBLISHER'S NOTE

Soon after the thirty-eight volumes forming *The Pelican Shake-speare* had been published, they were brought together in *The Complete Pelican Shakespeare*. The editorial revisions and new textual features are explained in detail in the General Editor's Preface to the one-volume edition. They have all been incorporated in the present volume. The following should be mentioned in particular:

The lines are not numbered in arbitrary units. Instead all lines are numbered which contain a word, phrase, or allusion explained in the glossarial notes. In the occasional instances where there is a long stretch of unannotated text, certain lines are numbered in italics to serve the conventional reference purpose.

The intrusive and often inaccurate place-headings inserted by early editors are omitted (as is becoming standard practise), but for the convenience of those who miss them, an indication of locale now appears as first item in the annotation of each scene.

In the interest of both elegance and utility, each speech-prefix is set in a separate line when the speaker's lines are in verse, except when these words form the second half of a pentameter line. Thus the verse form of the speech is kept visually intact, and turned-over lines are avoided. What is printed as verse and what is printed as prose has, in general, the authority of the original texts. Departures from the original texts in this regard have only the authority of editorial tradition and the judgment of the Pelican editors; and, in a few instances, are admittedly arbitrary.

SHAKESPEARE AND
HIS STAGE

William Shakespeare was christened in Holy Trinity Church, Stratford-upon-Avon, April 26, 1564. His birth is traditionally assigned to April 23. He was the eldest of four boys and two girls who survived infancy in the family of John Shakespeare, glover and trader of Henley Street, and his wife Mary Arden, daughter of a small landowner of Wilmcote. In 1568 John was elected Bailiff (equivalent to Mayor) of Stratford, having already filled the minor municipal offices. The town maintained for the sons of the burgesses a free school, taught by a university graduate and offering preparation in Latin sufficient for university entrance; its early registers are lost, but there can be little doubt that Shakespeare received the formal part of his education in this school.

On November 27, 1582, a license was issued for the marriage of William Shakespeare (aged eighteen) and Ann Hathaway (aged twenty-six), and on May 26, 1583, their child Susanna was christened in Holy Trinity Church. The inference that the marriage was forced upon the youth is natural but not inevitable; betrothal was legally binding at the time, and was sometimes regarded as conferring conjugal rights. Two additional children of the marriage, the twins Hamnet and Judith, were christened on February 2, 1585. Meanwhile the prosperity of the elder Shakespeares had declined, and William was impelled to seek a career outside Stratford.

The tradition that he spent some time as a country

7

teacher is old but unverifiable. Because of the absence of records his early twenties are called the "lost years," and only one thing about them is certain – that at least some of these years were spent in winning a place in the acting profession. He may have begun as a provincial trouper, but by 1592 he was established in London and prominent enough to be attacked. In a pamphlet of that year, *Groats-worth of Wit*, the ailing Robert Greene complained of the neglect which university writers like himself had suffered from actors, one of whom was daring to set up as a playwright:

... an vpstart Crow, beautified with our feathers, that with his *Tygers hart wrapt in a Players hyde*, supposes he is as well able to bombast out a blanke verse as the best of you: and beeing an absolute *Iohannes fac totum*, is in his owne conceit the onely Shake-scene in a countrey.

The pun on his name, and the parody of his line "O tiger's heart wrapped in a woman's hide" (*3 Henry VI*), pointed clearly to Shakespeare. Some of his admirers protested, and Henry Chettle, the editor of Greene's pamphlet, saw fit to apologize:

... I am as sory as if the originall fault had beene my fault, because my selfe haue seene his demeanor no lesse ciuill than he excelent in the qualitie he professes: Besides, diuers of worship haue reported his vprightnes of dealing, which argues his honesty, and his facetious grace in writting, that approoues his Art. (Prefatory epistle, *Kind-Harts Dreame*)

The plague closed the London theatres for many months in 1592–94, denying the actors their livelihood. To this period belong Shakespeare's two narrative poems, *Venus and Adonis* and *The Rape of Lucrece*, both dedicated to the Earl of Southampton. No doubt the poet was rewarded with a gift of money as usual in such cases, but he did no further dedicating and we have no reliable information on whether Southampton, or anyone else, became his regular patron. His sonnets, first mentioned in 1598 and published without his consent in 1609, are intimate without being

8

explicitly autobiographical. They seem to commemorate the poet's friendship with an idealized youth, rivalry with a more favored poet, and love affair with a dark mistress; and his bitterness when the mistress betrays him in conjunction with the friend; but it is difficult to decide precisely what the "story" is, impossible to decide whether it is fictional or true. The true distinction of the sonnets, at least of those not purely conventional, rests in the universality of the thoughts and moods they express, and in their poignancy and beauty.

In 1594 was formed the theatrical company known until 1603 as the Lord Chamberlain's men, thereafter as the King's men. Its original membership included, besides Shakespeare, the beloved clown Will Kempe and the famous actor Richard Burbage. The company acted in various London theatres and even toured the provinces, but it is chiefly associated in our minds with the Globe Theatre built on the south bank of the Thames in 1599. Shakespeare was an actor and joint owner of this company (and its Globe) through the remainder of his creative years. His plays, written at the average rate of two a year, together with Burbage's acting won it its place of leadership among the London companies.

Individual plays began to appear in print, in editions both honest and piratical, and the publishers became increasingly aware of the value of Shakespeare's name on the title pages. As early as 1598 he was hailed as the leading English dramatist in the *Palladis Tamia* of Francis Meres:

As *Plautus* and *Seneca* are accounted the best for Comedy and Tragedy among the Latines, so *Shakespeare* among the English is the most excellent in both kinds for the stage: for Comedy, witnes his *Gentlemen of Verona*, his *Errors*, his *Loue labors lost*, his *Loue labours wonne* [at one time in print but no longer extant, at least under this title], his *Midsummers night dream*, & his *Merchant of Venice*; for Tragedy, his *Richard the 2, Richard the 3, Henry the 4, King Iohn, Titus Andronicus*, and his *Romeo and Iuliet*.

The note is valuable both in indicating Shakespeare's prestige and in helping us to establish a chronology. In the second half of his writing career, history plays gave place to the great tragedies; and farces and light comedies gave place to the problem plays and symbolic romances. In 1623, seven years after his death, his former fellow-actors, John Heminge and Henry Condell, cooperated with a group of London printers in bringing out his plays in collected form. The volume is generally known as the First Folio.

Shakespeare had never severed his relations with Stratford. His wife and children may sometimes have shared his London lodgings, but their home was Stratford. His son Hamnet was buried there in 1596, and his daughters Susanna and Judith were married there in 1607 and 1616 respectively. (His father, for whom he had secured a coat of arms and thus the privilege of writing himself gentleman, died in 1601, his mother in 1608.) His considerable earnings in London, as actor-sharer, part owner of the Globe, and playwright, were invested chiefly in Stratford property. In 1597 he purchased for £60 New Place, one of the two most imposing residences in the town. A number of other business transactions, as well as minor episodes in his career, have left documentary records. By 1611 he was in a position to retire, and he seems gradually to have withdrawn from theatrical activity in order to live in Stratford. In March, 1616, he made a will, leaving token bequests to Burbage, Heminge, and Condell, but the bulk of his estate to his family. The most famous feature of the will, the bequest of the second-best bed to his wife, reveals nothing about Shakespeare's marriage; the quaintness of the provision seems commonplace to those familiar with ancient testaments. Shakespeare died April 23, 1616, and was buried in the Stratford church where he had been christened. Within seven years a monument was erected to his memory on the north wall of the chancel. Its portrait bust and the Droeshout engraving on the title page of the First Folio provide the only likenesses with an established claim to authenticity. The best verbal vignette was written by his rival Ben Jonson, the more impressive for being imbedded in a context mainly critical:

... I loved the man, and doe honour his memory (on this side idolatry) as much as any. Hee was indeed honest, and of an open and free nature: had an excellent Phantsie, brave notions, and gentle expressions.... (*Timber or Discoveries*, ca. 1623–30)

*

The reader of Shakespeare's plays is aided by a general knowledge of the way in which they were staged. The King's men acquired a roofed and artificially lighted theatre only toward the close of Shakespeare's career, and then only for winter use. Nearly all his plays were designed for performance in such structures as the Globe – a three-tiered amphitheatre with a large rectangular platform extending to the center of its yard. The plays were staged by daylight, by large casts brilliantly costumed, but with only a minimum of properties, without scenery, and quite possibly without intermissions. There was a rear stage gallery for action "above," and a curtained rear recess for "discoveries" and other special effects, but by far the major portion of any play was enacted upon the projecting platform, with episode following episode in swift succession, and with shifts of time and place signaled the audience only by the momentary clearing of the stage between the episodes. Information about the identity of the characters and, when necessary, about the time and place of the action was incorporated in the dialogue. No place-headings have been inserted in the present editions; these are apt to obscure the original fluidity of structure, with the emphasis upon action and speech rather than scenic background. (Indications of place are supplied in the footnotes.) The acting, including that of the youthful apprentices to the profession who performed the parts of women, was highly skillful, with a premium placed upon grace of gesture and beauty of diction. The audiences, a cross section of the general public, commonly numbered a thousand, sometimes more than two thousand. Judged by the type of plays they applauded, these audiences were not only large but also perceptive.

THE TEXTS OF THE PLAYS

About half of Shakespeare's plays appeared in print for the first time in the folio volume of 1623. The others had been published individually, usually in quarto volumes, during his lifetime or in the six years following his death. The copy used by the printers of the quartos varied greatly in merit, sometimes representing Shakespeare's true text, sometimes only a debased version of that text. The copy used by the printers of the folio also varied in merit, but was chosen with care. Since it consisted of the best available manuscripts, or the more acceptable quartos (although frequently in editions other than the first), or of quartos corrected by reference to manuscripts, we have good or reasonably good texts of most of the thirty-seven plays.

In the present series, the plays have been newly edited from quarto or folio texts, depending, when a choice offered, upon which is now regarded by bibliographical specialists as the more authoritative. The ideal has been to reproduce the chosen texts with as few alterations as possible, beyond occasional relineation, expansion of abbreviations, and modernization of punctuation and spelling. Emendation is held to a minimum, and such material as has been added, in the way of stage directions and lines supplied by an alternative text, has been enclosed in square brackets.

None of the plays printed in Shakespeare's lifetime were divided into acts and scenes, and the inference is that the author's own manuscripts were not so divided. In the folio collection, some of the plays remained undivided, some were divided into acts, and some were divided into acts and scenes. During the eighteenth century all of the plays were divided into acts and scenes, and in the Cambridge edition of the mid-nineteenth century, from which the influential Globe text derived, this division was more or less regularized and the lines were numbered. Many useful works of reference employ the act–scene–line apparatus thus established.

Since this act–scene division is obviously convenient, but is of very dubious authority so far as Shakespeare's own structural principles are concerned, or the original manner of staging his plays, a problem is presented to modern editors. In the present series the act–scene division is retained marginally, and may be viewed as a reference aid like the line numbering. A star marks the points of division when these points have been determined by a cleared stage indicating a shift of time and place in the action of the play, or when no harm results from the editorial assumption that there is such a shift. However, at those points where the established division is clearly misleading – that is, where continuous action has been split up into separate "scenes" – the star is omitted and the distortion corrected. This mechanical expedient seemed the best means of combining utility and accuracy.

THE GENERAL EDITOR

INTRODUCTION

Despite its apparent simplicity, this play has occasioned opposite interpretations. For some critics, Caesar is, in Antony's words, "the noblest man / That ever livèd in the tide of times" and the assassination a senseless act of criminal folly, while for others Caesar is an ambitious tyrant and the assassination a valiant attempt by patriotic Romans to preserve the Republic. These views of the play correspond to contrasting views of the historical events it dramatizes – the medieval condemnation of Brutus and Cassius, as in Dante and Chaucer, and the Renaissance condemnation of Caesar, as in Machiavelli, Elyot, Montaigne, Sidney, Marlowe, Harington, and Jonson. Shakespeare himself reflects the medieval view in his early trilogy on the reign of Henry VI and the Renaissance view in plays written in the late 1590's and after. As a practical dramatist, however, he was not concerned to teach his audience a particular interpretation of history, as he had to some extent been forced to do in his English chronicle plays; rather, he knew that the more and less educated members of his audience would tend to hold, respectively, the Renaissance and medieval views, and he chose to fashion his play in such a way that it should take advantage of the preconceptions of both sections of his audience. The result is a structure of sustained dramatic ambiguities that are resolved only in the latter part of the play, a method of construction that he was to use with even more brilliant and controversial effect in his next tragedy, *Hamlet*.

Julius Caesar was probably first produced at the new Globe Theatre in the fall of 1599, some months after the appearance of *Henry V*, the last of the nine English histories that Shakespeare wrote in the 1590's, and shortly before the appearance of a comedy with the significant title *As You Like It*. The history and the comedy are culminations of established interests on Shakespeare's part; *The Tragedy of Julius Caesar*, although Shakespeare had already written highly popular tragedies, is a new departure, an important turning-point midway in his career as England's most popular dramatist. He had abandoned English history, was soon to abandon romantic comedy, and was about to undertake his series of great heroic tragedies, to be framed, as it turned out, by four tragedies based on Sir Thomas North's translation of Plutarch's *Lives*, the literary source Shakespeare seems most to have respected and admired.

With *Julius Caesar* he turned for the first time from Holinshed's *Chronicles* of English history to Plutarch's comparative studies of the careers of great men of Greece and Rome. He was turning from English to Roman history for subject matter, but more significantly he was turning from history to tragedy. His earlier English histories had indeed been tragical, although the later ones must more aptly be termed comical, and they had finally to take an intensely patriotic view of the civil wars that led to the accession of Henry VII, the first of the Tudors. Even his other tragedies, unlike those drawn from Plutarch, end with the destruction of the forces of evil and the belated victory of the good forces that survive. The Plutarchan tragedies, particularly those concerned with the Roman civil wars, with the decline and fall of the Roman Republic, are more ironic; the forces that prevail at the ends of these tragedies cannot easily be seen as forces of good, and they are, in each case, forces hostile to the tragic heroes. For Brutus is the tragic hero of *Julius Caesar*; Caesar himself, or more properly "the spirit of Caesar" as embodied in Octavius, is the historic victor.

To men of the Renaissance, Republican Rome was the apex of human achievement in civilization and political organization, although without benefit of Christianity. Its heroes, whether legendary or historical, were held in reverence as notable examples of patriotism, military valor, and the pagan virtues. In his popular poem *The Rape of Lucrece* Shakespeare had written of two of the legendary figures, the chaste Lucrece and the patriot Junius Brutus, founder of the Republic and reputed ancestor of Marcus Brutus. In *Julius Caesar* the names of two other admired Romans, Pompey and Cato of Utica, are invoked to lend moral weight to the Republican cause, for both had been destroyed by Caesar as the renowned Cicero was to be destroyed by Caesar's followers.

The play opens with the tribunes of the people, whose function it was to safeguard and maintain popular liberties, using Pompey's memory to dissuade the fickle plebeians from participating in Caesar's triumph over fellow Romans; they express the Republican fear that Caesar seeks to rob the Romans of their ancient liberties. In the next scene, Caesar's ambition to be crowned, a move which if successful would reduce the Republic to a monarchy, is vividly communicated as an off-stage action accompanying Cassius' attempt to persuade Brutus to lead a conspiracy against Caesar. Caesar's scheme to have himself crowned by popular acclaim would surely have reminded many in Shakespeare's audience of the similar scheme used by the usurping tyrant Richard III, as Shakespeare had dramatized it. In both cases, the unwillingness of the people to go along with the scheme frustrates it, and the schemers must resort to other devices to get themselves crowned. The center of interest in this play, however, is not the progress of Caesar and his followers; it is the impact of "the spirit of Caesar" on his fellow Romans, particularly on Brutus, who must choose between his personal friendship for Caesar and his public responsibility, both as a Roman and as a praetor, to prevent the subversion of the Republic. This is his tragic dilemma and Shakespeare's major interest in the first two acts of the play.

Brutus, from the first, is "with himself at war" and deeply concerned for "the general good." His soliloquy at the beginning of Act II, the first of Shakespeare's famous deliberative soliloquies, dramatizes his attempt to resolve his inner conflict. The question is not whether or not Caesar must be killed for the general good – Brutus has already decided that he must be – but how Brutus can reconcile his political decision as a public man with his conscience as a private man: "I know no personal cause to spurn at him, / But for the general." In the rest of the soliloquy, as Coleridge failed to perceive but as Kittredge points out, Brutus considers Caesar as a private man and can find nothing to justify his assassination. By means of the commonplace, however, that absolute power usually corrupts absolutely, he is able to bring his personal feelings into line with his sense of public duty. Yet he is not comfortable with his decision – "all the interim is / Like a phantasma or a hideous dream" – and he continues to distinguish between Caesar the man and Caesar the would-be king and probable tyrant:

> Let's be sacrificers, but not butchers, Caius.
> We all stand up against the spirit of Caesar,
> And in the spirit of men there is no blood.
> O that we then could come by Caesar's spirit
> And not dismember Caesar! But, alas,
> Caesar must bleed for it.

That is what he says privately to the other conspirators; it is an essential part of his public explanation to the plebeians in the Forum: "Not that I loved Caesar less, but that I loved Rome more. . . . As Caesar loved me, I weep for him; . . . as he was ambitious, I slew him."

Cassius and Antony, unlike Brutus, are unscrupulous politicians of the sort that the Elizabethans called Machiavellian. Both place personal gain above the general good. They are, respectively, the dominant villains of the first and second halves of the play. Cassius' soliloquy at the end of Act I, scene ii, is quite as much like the soliloquies of Iago as is Antony's brief soliloquy after he has delivered his masterpiece of demagogic rhetoric: "Now let it work. Mischief, thou art afoot, / Take thou what course thou wilt." Cassius, for all his political shrewdness, must defer to Brutus – as Antony must later defer to Octavius – since Brutus had been chosen to lead the conspiracy just because his known integrity, "like richest alchemy," would make it seem worthy and virtuous. Plutarch analyzes Brutus' failure to preserve the Republic as the result of two major political "mistakes": his refusal to kill Caesar's chief supporters, notably Antony, along with Caesar, and his permission that Antony speak at Caesar's funeral. Some critics find a third "mistake" in Brutus' decision to meet the enemy at Philippi instead of letting them search out the Republican forces. Shakespeare has Cassius propose shrewder alternatives to each of these choices, but in each case Cassius is a foil to Brutus, whose nobility as tragic hero is only the more enhanced by his rejections of Cassius' politic proposals.

The one episode in which Cassius passionately stands up to Brutus, though he is as usual overridden by him, is the famous quarrel scene in Act IV. Here Brutus is most nearly disillusioned about the motives of his fellow conspirators:

> Did not great Julius bleed for justice sake?
> What villain touched his body that did stab
> And not for justice? What, shall one of us,
> That struck the foremost man of all this world
> But for supporting robbers – shall we now
> Contaminate our fingers with base bribes...?

Shakespeare has shown us, at the beginning of Act IV, those robbers, the triumvirate, about their work, with Antony cast in the most villainous role of the three. Many in Shakespeare's audience must have been reminded of the proverbial lack of honor among thieves, which finally, as Shakespeare was to dramatize it in *Antony and Cleopatra*, works to the advantage of Octavius Caesar, the coldest, youngest, and most cunning of the three. In this play, Octavius overrides Antony, much as Brutus overrides Cassius, and the fact that Octavius is given the final speech of the play, generally assigned in both the tragedies and the histories to the highest-ranking of the surviving figures, foreshadows his defeat of Antony.

Antony is at least capable of feeling, and his lamentation over the corpse of Caesar makes him highly sympathetic in Act III, scene i. He and Cassius are opposite types, both of them foils for Brutus, who in some respects stands as a mean between their extremes. Antony is too "gamesome," "a masker and a reveller," and far from having Cassius' "lean and hungry look." Cassius "loves no plays," "hears no music," "reads much," and is envious. They are, respectively, excessive and deficient in their capacities for feeling, for "love," one of the key-words of the play. Brutus loves, and inspires love in others :

> My heart doth joy that yet in all my life
> I found no man but he was true to me.

Like Cassius he reads, like Antony he loves music, but he is not dissolute like the latter, nor envious like the former. His integrity, his honor, contrasts sharply with the conniving of Antony and Cassius. His love for Portia and his concern for the welfare of his servants (notably Lucius, who has no counterpart in Plutarch) heighten our sympathetic admiration of him. Antony's final speech in praise of Brutus directs our proper response to the tragic hero defeated by the spirit of Caesar :

This was the noblest Roman of them all.
All the conspirators save only he
Did that they did in envy of great Caesar;
He, only in a general honest thought
And common good to all, made one of them.

Caesar himself is almost enigmatic. Brutus, after the assassination, calls him "the foremost man of all this world," yet Shakespeare presents him in his own person as a pompous, arrogant usurper, and in Cassius' description as a Colossus afflicted with unmanly weaknesses. He sees himself as the polestar and as Mount Olympus, yet he is associated with sterility, epilepsy, and deafness. He insists that he is unshakeable, yet Cassius tells us "How he did shake" and we see how he is shaken. Cassius sees him as a wolf, ferociously carnivorous, Antony as a hart, harmlessly herbivorous. Other images are applied to him, but the concept of Caesar as a diseased statue is the most powerful in the first movement of the play, where he is not so much an active force for evil as a static center of corruption. Even many of the medieval glorifiers of Caesar condemned him for the inordinate ambition that led to his assassination and the ultimate decline of Rome. Even the majority of Renaissance glorifiers of Brutus recognized Caesar's earlier greatness while condemning him for the subversion of the Republic. Shakespeare, while he is careful to disabuse his audience of the vulgar error that Caesar was actually the first of the Roman Emperors, gives the spirit of Caesar its historical due, but he seems to have thought to show Caesar himself as a victim of that blind infatuation, "security," that leads great men to their destruction. Caesar's *hubris* is more extraordinary than that of any other major figure in Shakespeare's plays.

After Brutus, Caesar, Cassius, and Antony, the plebeians are the most important "character" in the play. It is their corruption that defeats the Republican cause from the start. Brutus' major disillusionment, if this had been a history play, should have occurred at the very moment of his greatest apparent success – the moment when, after his plain and honest speech in the Forum, the plebeians shout "Let him be Caesar." "Caesar's better parts / Shall be crowned in Brutus." At this point Shakespeare's audience knew that the Roman mob was no longer capable of Republicanism, that the Romans, like themselves, might best be governed by a king. It is Brutus' nobility as a tragic hero, and his weakness as a political leader, not to have perceived this fact, of which Antony and Octavius will take such advantage. Yet the less politic Brutus is, the more heroic he can be made. Indeed Shakespeare, in transmuting the material he found in Plutarch's lives of Caesar, Antony, and Brutus, selected from and augmented that material in such a way as to make Brutus his centrally admirable figure, the high-minded man in a corrupt world.

Julius Caesar has been widely acclaimed for its essential truth to the spirit of ancient Rome, despite such evident anachronisms as chimney tops, striking clocks, and books with leaves. The contrast between Stoicism and Epicureanism, two of the dominant philosophic systems of the Romans, is clearly brought out. In fact, it is Cassius' shift from Epicureanism (which to the Elizabethans meant atheism) to a belief in portents that helps to make him a sympathetic figure at the end of the play. The anachronisms are not important. To the Elizabethans, excepting such purists as Ben Jonson, the play must have seemed pretty thoroughly Roman. Although there are certain homely references to details of costume that can only have been Elizabethan, there was probably, as we can surmise from a contemporary illustration of the staging of *Titus Andronicus*, an attempt to clothe the major figures in costumes that the Elizabethans thought of as Roman.

Even the style of the play seems to reflect a similar intention. It is unusually straightforward, having neither the lyric floridity of the earlier tragedies nor the condensed

21

metaphoric texture of the later plays. The animal and hunting imagery is as forthright in its application as the frequent use of monosyllabic lines is forceful in its simplicity. Shakespeare subordinated poetry to rhetoric to gain his Roman effects. Rhetoric, the art of persuasion, is structural as well as stylistic in this play: the tribunes persuade the people not to honor Caesar, Cassius persuades Brutus to lead the conspiracy, Brutus persuades himself of the justice of his cause, Portia persuades Brutus to reveal his secret to her, Calphurnia persuades Caesar not to go forth, Decius persuades him to go, Brutus persuades the people to support the Republicans. Antony persuades them to mutiny. This persuasion and counter-persuasion reaches its climax with the speeches in the Forum, the turning-point of the play, after which the spirit of Caesar dominates and the Republic, along with the Republicans, is destroyed.

Shakespeare compresses events of three years into five dramatic "days," the first two of which account for the first three acts of the play, and he compresses the complexities of motives, as Plutarch discussed them, in order to gain momentum for his powerful rhetorical construction. Despite this compression, Shakespeare, following Plutarch, is concerned less with what happens than with why it happens, less with events than with interacting purposes, and this remains his major interest in his later plays. *Julius Caesar* never mounts to the passionate intensity of the greater tragedies that followed it – in this respect it is more stoically Roman than they – but it anticipates their pattern of heroic disillusionment, inner conflict, and the attempt to set right a time which is out of joint. Unlike his legendary ancestor, Junius Brutus, and unlike his immediate successor, Hamlet, Brutus does not accomplish his purpose. Elizabethans may have seen the triumph of Caesarism as Plutarch saw it – "the state of Rome (in my opinion) . . . could not more abide to be governed by many lords, but required one only absolute governor" – or even as an Elizabethan publisher saw it – "an evident demonstration that peoples' rule must give place, and Prince's power prevail." As the play presents it, however, the triumph of Caesarism is a matter of history making tragedy ironic. There is no restoration of a positive moral order to relieve the sense of tragic waste. Only the memory of Brutus' nobility, as his corpse is carried off, transcends the bleak facts of history at the end of the play:

> His life was gentle, and the elements
> So mixed in him that Nature might stand up
> And say to all the world, 'This was a man!'

Columbia University   S. F. JOHNSON

NOTE ON THE TEXT

Julius Caesar was first published in the folio of 1623, evidently from the playhouse prompt-book or a careful transcript of it. The folio text is divided into acts but not into scenes. The act–scene division supplied marginally for reference in the present edition is that of the later editors, and it needlessly indicates a break in the action at IV, iii, 1. The action in V, here printed continuously as in the folio, takes place in various parts of the plains of Philippi. Certain character names have here been normalized in the text as well as in speech-prefixes:

I, i, s.d. *Marullus* (F Murellus)
I, ii, s.d. *Marullus* (F Murellus)   282 *Marullus* (F Murrellus)
     3, 4, 6, 190 *Antonius* (F Antonio)
I, iii, 37 *Antonius* (F Antonio)
III, i, 275 s.d. *Octavius* (F Octavio)
IV, iii, 242, 244, 244 s.d., 289 *Claudius* (F Claudio)   244, 244 s.d.,
     289 *Varro* (F Varrus)
V, ii, 4 *Octavius* (F Octavio)
V, iii, 108 *Labeo, Flavius* (F Labio, Flavio)

Throughout the play Caska is changed to *Casca*, and Lucillius to *Lucilius*. Otherwise the present edition adheres closely to the folio text, and admits only the following emendations in addition to the correction of obvious typographical errors. The adopted reading in italics is followed by the folio reading in roman.

I, iii, 129 *fet'rous* Fauors
II, i, 40 *ides* first
II, ii, 19 *fought* fight   23 *did neigh* do neigh   46 *are* heare
III, i, 113 *states* State   115 *lies* lye   283 *for* from
III, ii, 104 *art* are
V, iii, 104 *Thasos* Tharsus
V, iv, 17 *the news* thee news
V, v, 33 *to thee too, Strato. Countrymen,* to thee, to Strato, Countreymen:

JULIUS CAESAR

Julius Caesar
Octavius Caesar ⎫
Marcus Antonius ⎬ *triumvirs after the death of*
M. Aemilius Lepidus ⎭ *Julius Caesar*
Cicero ⎫
Publius ⎬ *senators*
Popilius Lena ⎭
Marcus Brutus ⎫
Cassius ⎪
Casca ⎪
Trebonius ⎬ *conspirators against*
Ligarius ⎪ *Julius Caesar*
Decius Brutus ⎪
Metellus Cimber ⎪
Cinna ⎭
Flavius and Marullus, tribunes of the people
Artemidorus, a teacher of rhetoric
A Soothsayer
Cinna, a poet
Another Poet
Lucilius ⎫
Titinius ⎪
Messala ⎬ *friends to Brutus and Cassius*
Young Cato ⎪
Volumnius ⎭
Varro ⎫
Clitus ⎪
Claudius ⎪
Strato ⎬ *servants to Brutus*
Lucius ⎪
Dardanius ⎭
Pindarus, servant to Cassius
A Servant to Caesar ; to Antony ; to Octavius
Calphurnia, wife to Caesar
Portia, wife to Brutus
The Ghost of Caesar
Senators, Citizens, Guards, Attendants, &c.

Scene: *Rome ; near Sardis ; near Philippi*]

Enter Flavius, Marullus, and certain Commoners   I, i
over the stage.

FLAVIUS

Hence! home, you idle creatures, get you home!
Is this a holiday? What, know you not,
Being mechanical, you ought not walk   3
Upon a laboring day without the sign   4
Of your profession? Speak, what trade art thou?

CARPENTER Why, sir, a carpenter.

MARULLUS

Where is thy leather apron and thy rule?
What dost thou with thy best apparel on?
You, sir, what trade are you?

COBBLER Truly, sir, in respect of a fine workman I am   10
but, as you would say, a cobbler.   11

MARULLUS

But what trade art thou? Answer me directly.   12

COBBLER A trade, sir, that I hope I may use with a safe
conscience, which is indeed, sir, a mender of bad soles.   14

FLAVIUS

What trade, thou knave? Thou naughty knave, what   15
trade?

I, i A street in Rome   s.d. *over the stage* who cross the stage before halting
3 *mechanical* workers   4 *sign* tools and costume (which indicate a man's
trade)   10 *in . . . workman* as far as skilled work is concerned   11 *cobbler*
(with pun on 'bungler')   12 *directly* plainly   14 *soles* (with pun on 'souls')
15 *naughty* worthless

16 COBBLER Nay, I beseech you, sir, be not out with me.
17   Yet if you be out, sir, I can mend you.

MARULLUS
     What mean'st thou by that? Mend me, thou saucy
        fellow?

COBBLER Why, sir, cobble you.

FLAVIUS
     Thou art a cobbler, art thou?

COBBLER Truly, sir, all that I live by is with the awl. I
22   meddle with no tradesman's matters nor women's mat-
23   ters; but withal – I am indeed, sir, a surgeon to old shoes.
24   When they are in great danger, I recover them. As proper
25   men as ever trod upon neat's leather have gone upon my
        handiwork.

FLAVIUS
     But wherefore art not in thy shop to-day?
     Why dost thou lead these men about the streets?

COBBLER Truly, sir, to wear out their shoes, to get my-
        self into more work. But indeed, sir, we make holiday to
31   see Caesar and to rejoice in his triumph.

MARULLUS
     Wherefore rejoice? What conquest brings he home?
33   What tributaries follow him to Rome
     To grace in captive bonds his chariot wheels?
     You blocks, you stones, you worse than senseless
        things!
     O you hard hearts, you cruel men of Rome.
37   Knew you not Pompey? Many a time and oft
     Have you climbed up to walls and battlements,
     To tow'rs and windows, yea, to chimney tops,
     Your infants in your arms, and there have sat
     The livelong day, with patient expectation,

16 *out* angry   17 *be out* have worn-out shoes; *mend* (with pun on 'reform')
22 *meddle* (with pun on 'am intimate')   23 *withal* nevertheless (with puns
on 'all' and 'awl')   24 *recover* re-sole (with pun on 'cure'); *proper* hand-
some   25 *neat's* cattle's (the phrase is proverbial); *gone* walked   31 *triumph*
victory procession   33 *tributaries* captives   37 *Pompey* (defeated by
Caesar in 48 B.C., later murdered)

28

To see great Pompey pass the streets of Rome.
And when you saw his chariot but appear,
Have you not made an universal shout,
That Tiber trembled underneath her banks   45
To hear the replication of your sounds   46
Made in her concave shores?   47
And do you now put on your best attire?
And do you now cull out a holiday?
And do you now strew flowers in his way
That comes in triumph over Pompey's blood?   51
Be gone!
Run to your houses, fall upon your knees,
Pray to the gods to intermit the plague   54
That needs must light on this ingratitude.

FLAVIUS

Go, go, good countrymen, and for this fault
Assemble all the poor men of your sort;
Draw them to Tiber banks, and weep your tears
Into the channel, till the lowest stream
Do kiss the most exalted shores of all.   60

            Exeunt all the Commoners.

See, whe'r their basest mettle be not moved.   61
They vanish tongue-tied in their guiltiness.
Go you down that way towards the Capitol;
This way will I. Disrobe the images   64
If you do find them decked with ceremonies.   65

MARULLUS

May we do so?
You know it is the feast of Lupercal.   67

FLAVIUS

It is no matter. Let no images

---

45 *That* such that   46 *replication* reverberation   47 *concave shores* hollowed-out banks   51 *blood* i.e. sons (also the blood of Pompey and his followers)   54 *intermit* withhold   60 *most exalted shores* highest flood level, verge of heavens   61 *whe'r* whether; *their basest* even their very base; *mettle* substance, temperament   64 *images* statues   65 *ceremonies* ornaments   67 *Lupercal* fertility festival held on February 15

69 Be hung with Caesar's trophies. I'll about
70 And drive away the vulgar from the streets.
    So do you too, where you perceive them thick.
    These growing feathers plucked from Caesar's wing
73 Will make him fly an ordinary pitch,
74 Who else would soar above the view of men
    And keep us all in servile fearfulness.   *Exeunt.*

*

I, ii   *[Music.] Enter Caesar, Antony (for the course),*
               Calphurnia, Portia, Decius, Cicero, Brutus,
               Cassius, Casca, [a great crowd following, among
               them] a Soothsayer; after them, Marullus and
               Flavius.

CAESAR
    Calphurnia.
CASCA   Peace, ho! Caesar speaks.
               [Music ceases.]
CAESAR   Calphurnia.
CALPHURNIA
    Here, my lord.
CAESAR
    Stand you directly in Antonius' way
4   When he doth run his course. Antonius.
ANTONY
    Caesar, my lord?
CAESAR
    Forget not in your speed, Antonius,
    To touch Calphurnia; for our elders say
    The barren, touchèd in this holy chase,
    Shake off their sterile curse.

69 *trophies* ornaments   70 *vulgar* plebeians, common people   73 *pitch*
height   74 *above...men* i.e. like the gods
I, ii A public place   4 *run his course* i.e. race naked through the city striking
bystanders with a goatskin thong

ANTONY   I shall remember.
   When Caesar says 'Do this,' it is performed.

CAESAR
   Set on, and leave no ceremony out.
      [Music.]

SOOTHSAYER   Caesar!

CAESAR   Ha! Who calls?

CASCA
   Bid every noise be still. Peace yet again!
      [Music ceases.]

CAESAR
   Who is it in the press that calls on me?   15
   I hear a tongue shriller than all the music
   Cry 'Caesar!' Speak. Caesar is turned to hear.

SOOTHSAYER
   Beware the ides of March.   18

CAESAR   What man is that?

BRUTUS
   A soothsayer bids you beware the ides of March.

CAESAR
   Set him before me; let me see his face.

CASSIUS
   Fellow, come from the throng; look upon Caesar.

CAESAR
   What say'st thou to me now? Speak once again.

SOOTHSAYER
   Beware the ides of March.

CAESAR
   He is a dreamer. Let us leave him. Pass.   24
         Sennet. Exeunt. Mane[n]t Brutus and Cassius.

CASSIUS
   Will you go see the order of the course?   25

BRUTUS   Not I.

CASSIUS   I pray you do.

---

15 *press* crowd   18 *ides* the half-way point in the month, the fifteenth day in March, May, July, and October   24 s.d. *Sennet* trumpet call   25 *order* events

BRUTUS

28   I am not gamesome. I do lack some part
29   Of that quick spirit that is in Antony.
     Let me not hinder, Cassius, your desires.
     I'll leave you.

CASSIUS

     Brutus, I do observe you now of late ;
33   I have not from your eyes that gentleness
34   And show of love as I was wont to have.
35   You bear too stubborn and too strange a hand
     Over your friend that loves you.

BRUTUS   Cassius,

37   Be not deceived. If I have veiled my look,
     I turn the trouble of my countenance
39   Merely upon myself. Vexèd I am
40   Of late with passions of some difference,
41   Conceptions only proper to myself,
42   Which give some soil, perhaps, to my behaviors ;
     But let not therefore my good friends be grieved
     (Among which number, Cassius, be you one)
45   Nor construe any further my neglect
     Than that poor Brutus, with himself at war,
47   Forgets the shows of love to other men.

CASSIUS

48   Then, Brutus, I have much mistook your passion ;
49   By means whereof this breast of mine hath buried
     Thoughts of great value, worthy cogitations.
     Tell me, good Brutus, can you see your face ?

BRUTUS

     No, Cassius ; for the eye sees not itself
     But by reflection, by some other things.

---

28 *gamesome* sport-loving   29 *quick spirit* lively nature   33 *gentleness* well-bred politeness   34 *love* friendship; *wont* accustomed   35–36 *bear . . . Over* behave roughly and unnaturally to   37 *veiled my look* i.e. concealed my true friendship   39 *Merely* wholly   40 *passions . . . difference* conflicting emotions   41 *proper to* concerning   42 *soil* blemish   45 *construe* interpret (accent on first syllable)   47 *shows* manifestations   48 *passion* feelings   49 *buried* concealed

CASSIUS 'Tis just.   54
   And it is very much lamented, Brutus,
   That you have no such mirrors as will turn   56
   Your hidden worthiness into your eye,   57
   That you might see your shadow. I have heard   58
   Where many of the best respect in Rome   59
   (Except immortal Caesar), speaking of Brutus
   And groaning underneath this age's yoke,
   Have wished that noble Brutus had his eyes.

BRUTUS
   Into what dangers would you lead me, Cassius,
   That you would have me seek into myself
   For that which is not in me?

CASSIUS
   Therefore, good Brutus, be prepared to hear;
   And since you know you cannot see yourself
   So well as by reflection, I, your glass,   68
   Will modestly discover to yourself   69
   That of yourself which you yet know not of.
   And be not jealous on me, gentle Brutus.   71
   Were I a common laughter, or did use   72
   To stale with ordinary oaths my love   73
   To every new protester; if you know   74
   That I do fawn on men and hug them hard,
   And after scandal them; or if you know   76
   That I profess myself in banqueting   77
   To all the rout, then hold me dangerous.   78
     Flourish and shout.

BRUTUS
   What means this shouting? I do fear the people
   Choose Caesar for their king.

---

54 *just* true **56** *turn* reflect **57** *hidden worthiness* true nobility, inner worth **58** *shadow* image **59** *best respect* highest repute **68** *glass* mirror **69** *modestly* without exaggeration **71** *jealous on* suspicious of **72** *laughter* object of ridicule; *did use* were accustomed **73** *stale* cheapen; *ordinary* tavern (?), commonplace (?) **74** *protester* one who easily declares friendship **76** *scandal* slander **77** *profess myself* declare my friendship **78** *rout* rabble **s.d.** *Flourish* elaborate trumpet call

CASSIUS   Ay, do you fear it ?
   Then must I think you would not have it so.
BRUTUS
   I would not, Cassius ; yet I love him well.
   But wherefore do you hold me here so long ?
   What is it that you would impart to me ?
85 If it be aught toward the general good,
   Set honor in one eye and death i' th' other,
87 And I will look on both indifferently ;
88 For let the gods so speed me as I love
   The name of honor more than I fear death.
CASSIUS
   I know that virtue to be in you, Brutus,
91 As well as I do know your outward favor.
   Well, honor is the subject of my story.
   I cannot tell what you and other men
94 Think of this life ; but for my single self,
95 I had as lief not be as live to be
96 In awe of such a thing as I myself.
   I was born free as Caesar ; so were you.
   We both have fed as well, and we can both
   Endure the winter's cold as well as he.
   For once, upon a raw and gusty day,
101 The troubled Tiber chafing with her shores,
   Caesar said to me, 'Dar'st thou, Cassius, now
   Leap in with me into this angry flood
   And swim to yonder point ?' Upon the word,
105 Accoutred as I was, I plungèd in
   And bade him follow. So indeed he did.
   The torrent roared, and we did buffet it
   With lusty sinews, throwing it aside
109 And stemming it with hearts of controversy.

---

85 *general good* welfare of the state   87 *indifferently* impartially   88 *speed me* make me prosper   91 *favor* appearance   94 *single* particular   95 *as lief* . . . *as* rather than   96 *such . . . myself* i.e. a mere mortal   101 *chafing with* raging against   105 *Accoutred* fully armed   109 *stemming . . . controversy* making headway with keen competition

But ere we could arrive the point proposed,   110
Caesar cried, 'Help me, Cassius, or I sink!'
I, as Aeneas, our great ancestor,   112
Did from the flames of Troy upon his shoulder
The old Anchises bear, so from the waves of Tiber
Did I the tirèd Caesar. And this man
Is now become a god, and Cassius is
A wretched creature and must bend his body
If Caesar carelessly but nod on him.
He had a fever when he was in Spain,
And when the fit was on him, I did mark   120
How he did shake. 'Tis true, this god did shake.
His coward lips did from their color fly,   122
And that same eye whose bend doth awe the world   123
Did lose his luster. I did hear him groan.   124
Ay, and that tongue of his that bade the Romans
Mark him and write his speeches in their books,
'Alas,' it cried, 'give me some drink, Titinius,'
As a sick girl! Ye gods, it doth amaze me
A man of such a feeble temper should   129
So get the start of the majestic world   130
And bear the palm alone.   131
        Shout. Flourish.

BRUTUS
    Another general shout?
    I do believe that these applauses are
    For some new honors that are heaped on Caesar.

CASSIUS
    Why, man, he doth bestride the narrow world
    Like a Colossus, and we petty men   136
    Walk under his huge legs and peep about
    To find ourselves dishonorable graves.

110 *arrive* attain   112 *Aeneas* founder of the Roman state and hero of
Virgil's *Aeneid*; Anchises was his father   120 *fit* periodic chills; *mark*
observe   122 *color* i.e. the color fled from his lips like cowardly soldiers
deserting their flag   123 *bend* glance   124 *his* its   129 *temper* consti-
tution   130 *get the start of* outstrip all others in   131 *palm* victor's prize
136 *Colossus* gigantic statue; *petty* inconsiderable

35

139 Men at some time are masters of their fates.
   The fault, dear Brutus, is not in our stars,
   But in ourselves, that we are underlings.
   'Brutus,' and 'Caesar.' What should be in that 'Caesar'?
143 Why should that name be sounded more than yours?
   Write them together: yours is as fair a name.
   Sound them: it doth become the mouth as well.
   Weigh them: it is as heavy. Conjure with 'em:
147 'Brutus' will start a spirit as soon as 'Caesar.'
   Now in the names of all the gods at once,
   Upon what meat doth this our Caesar feed
   That he is grown so great? Age, thou art shamed.
   Rome, thou hast lost the breed of noble bloods.
152 When went there by an age since the great Flood
   But it was famed with more than with one man?
   When could they say (till now) that talked of Rome
155 That her wide walks encompassed but one man?
156 Now is it Rome indeed, and room enough,
   When there is in it but one only man.
   O, you and I have heard our fathers say
159 There was a Brutus once that would have brooked
160 Th' eternal devil to keep his state in Rome
161 As easily as a king.

BRUTUS
162 That you do love me I am nothing jealous.
163 What you would work me to, I have some aim.
   How I have thought of this, and of these times,
   I shall recount hereafter. For this present,
166 I would not so (with love I might entreat you)
   Be any further moved. What you have said

139 *some* a particular 143 *sounded* pronounced (with pun on 'proclaimed')
147 *start* raise up 152 *Flood* Deucalion's flood, the classical analogue to
Noah's 155 *walks* parks and gardens surrounding ancient Rome 156
Rome, room (homonyms) 159 *a Brutus* Lucius Junius Brutus, founder of
the Roman Republic in 509 B.C.; *brooked* tolerated 160 *eternal* i.e. eternally
damned; *devil* (pronounced 'deil'); *his* the devil's 161 *As . . . king* as soon
as tolerate a king's doing so 162 *am nothing jealous* have no doubt 163
work persuade; *aim* idea 166 *so* that way

36

I will consider; what you have to say
I will with patience hear, and find a time
Both meet to hear and answer such high things.   170
Till then, my noble friend, chew upon this: 171
Brutus had rather be a villager
Than to repute himself a son of Rome
Under these hard conditions as this time   174
Is like to lay upon us.

CASSIUS   I am glad
That my weak words have struck but thus much show
Of fire from Brutus.   177
Enter Caesar and his Train.

BRUTUS
The games are done, and Caesar is returning.

CASSIUS
As they pass by, pluck Casca by the sleeve,
And he will (after his sour fashion) tell you   180
What hath proceeded worthy note to-day.

BRUTUS
I will do so. But look you, Cassius,
The angry spot doth glow on Caesar's brow,
And all the rest look like a chidden train.
Calphurnia's cheek is pale, and Cicero
Looks with such ferret and such fiery eyes   186
As we have seen him in the Capitol,
Being crossed in conference by some senators.   188

CASSIUS
Casca will tell us what the matter is.

CAESAR Antonius.
ANTONY Caesar?
CAESAR
Let me have men about me that are fat,   192
Sleek-headed men, and such as sleep a-nights.   193

---

170 *meet* fitting; *high* serious   171 *chew upon* consider   174 *these* such
177 s.d. *Train* followers   180 *sour* harsh   186 *ferret* like those of a ferret,
a weasel-like animal with red eyes   188 *crossed* opposed; *conference* debate
192 *fat* plump (not 'obese')   193 *Sleek-headed* well-groomed

194 Yond Cassius has a lean and hungry look.
     He thinks too much. Such men are dangerous.

ANTONY

     Fear him not, Caesar; he's not dangerous.
197 He is a noble Roman, and well given.

CAESAR

     Would he were fatter! But I fear him not.
199 Yet if my name were liable to fear,
     I do not know the man I should avoid
     So soon as that spare Cassius. He reads much,
     He is a great observer, and he looks
203 Quite through the deeds of men. He loves no plays
204 As thou dost, Antony; he hears no music.
205 Seldom he smiles, and smiles in such a sort
     As if he mocked himself and scorned his spirit
     That could be moved to smile at anything.
     Such men as he be never at heart's ease
     Whiles they behold a greater than themselves,
     And therefore are they very dangerous.
     I rather tell thee what is to be feared
     Than what I fear; for always I am Caesar.
     Come on my right hand, for this ear is deaf,
     And tell me truly what thou think'st of him.

                    Sennet. Exeunt Caesar and his Train.
                    [Manet Casca.]

CASCA

     You pulled me by the cloak. Would you speak with me?

BRUTUS

     Ay, Casca. Tell us what hath chanced to-day
217 That Caesar looks so sad.

CASCA

     Why, you were with him, were you not?

---

194 *lean* (proverbially associated with envy) 197 *given* disposed 199 *my name ... to* I were capable of 203 *through ... men* i.e. to the motivations behind men's actions 204 *hears no music* (cf. *Merchant of Venice*, V, i, 83–88: 'The man that hath no music in himself ... Is fit for treasons .... Let no such man be trusted.') 205 *sort* manner 217 *sad* serious

BRUTUS
I should not then ask Casca what had chanced.

CASCA Why, there was a crown offered him; and being offered him, he put it by with the back of his hand thus; and then the people fell a-shouting.

BRUTUS What was the second noise for?

CASCA Why, for that too.

CASSIUS
They shouted thrice. What was the last cry for?

CASCA Why, for that too.

BRUTUS Was the crown offered him thrice?

CASCA Ay, marry, was't! and he put it by thrice, every   228
time gentler than other; and at every putting-by mine
honest neighbors shouted.   230

CASSIUS
Who offered him the crown?

CASCA   Why, Antony.

BRUTUS
Tell us the manner of it, gentle Casca.   233

CASCA I can as well be hanged as tell the manner of it. It
was mere foolery; I did not mark it. I saw Mark Antony
offer him a crown – yet 'twas not a crown neither, 'twas
one of these coronets – and, as I told you, he put it by   237
once; but for all that, to my thinking, he would fain   238
have had it. Then he offered it to him again; then he put
it by again; but to my thinking, he was very loath to lay
his fingers off it. And then he offered it the third time.
He put it the third time by; and still as he refused it, the 242
rabblement hooted, and clapped their chopt hands, and   243
threw up their sweaty nightcaps, and uttered such a deal   244
of stinking breath because Caesar refused the crown that
it had, almost, choked Caesar; for he swounded and fell   246
down at it. And for mine own part, I durst not laugh, for

228 *marry* indeed (originally an oath by the Virgin Mary)   230 *honest*
worthy   233 *gentle* noble   237 *coronets* small crowns wreathed with
laurel   238 *fain* willingly   242 *still* each time   243 *chopt* chapped
244 *nightcaps* i.e. the citizens' caps (contemptuous)   246 *swounded* fainted

FEIGNED SICKNESS TO CROWD

fear of opening my lips and receiving the bad air.

CASSIUS

249 But soft, I pray you. What, did Caesar swound?

CASCA He fell down in the market place and foamed at
mouth and was speechless.

BRUTUS

252 'Tis very like he hath the falling sickness.

CASSIUS

No, Caesar hath it not; but you, and I,
254 And honest Casca, we have the falling sickness.

CASCA I know not what you mean by that, but I am sure
256 Caesar fell down. If the tag-rag people did not clap him
and hiss him, according as he pleased and displeased
258 them, as they use to do the players in the theatre, I am
no true man.

BRUTUS

What said he when he came unto himself?

CASCA Marry, before he fell down, when he perceived the
262 common herd was glad he refused the crown, he plucked
263 me ope his doublet and offered them his throat to cut.
264 An I had been a man of any occupation, if I would not
have taken him at a word I would I might go to hell
among the rogues. And so he fell. When he came to
himself again, he said, if he had done or said anything
amiss, he desired their worships to think it was his
infirmity. Three or four wenches where I stood cried
'Alas, good soul!' and forgave him with all their hearts.
But there's no heed to be taken of them. If Caesar had
stabbed their mothers, they would have done no less.

BRUTUS

273 And after that, he came thus sad away?

CASCA Ay.

---

249 *soft* slowly   **252** *like* likely that (Plutarch suggests Caesar feigned an
attack); *falling sickness* epilepsy   **254** *we . . . sickness* i.e. we are declining
(into subjection)   **256** *tag-rag people* ragged rabble   **258** *use* are accustomed
262–63 *plucked me* i.e. plucked (a colloquialism)   **263** *doublet* short jacket
264 *An* if; *man . . . occupation* workingman (also 'man of action'?)   **273**
sad seriously

CASSIUS
Did Cicero say anything?

CASCA Ay, he spoke Greek.

CASSIUS To what effect?

CASCA Nay, an I tell you that, I'll ne'er look you i' th'
face again. But those that understood him smiled at one
another and shook their heads; but for mine own part,
it was Greek to me. I could tell you more news too.
Marullus and Flavius, for pulling scarfs off Caesar's
images, are put to silence. Fare you well. There was more 283
foolery yet, if I could remember it.

CASSIUS Will you sup with me to-night, Casca?

CASCA No, I am promised forth.   286

CASSIUS Will you dine with me to-morrow?

CASCA Ay, if I be alive, and your mind hold, and your   288
dinner worth eating.

CASSIUS Good. I will expect you.

CASCA Do so. Farewell both.   *Exit.*

BRUTUS
What a blunt fellow is this grown to be!
He was quick mettle when he went to school.   293

CASSIUS
So is he now in execution
Of any bold or noble enterprise,
However he puts on this tardy form.   296
This rudeness is a sauce to his good wit,   297
Which gives men stomach to disgest his words   298
With better appetite.

BRUTUS
And so it is. For this time I will leave you.
To-morrow, if you please to speak with me,
I will come home to you; or if you will,   302

283 *put to silence* deprived of their tribuneships and exiled (?) or executed
(?) (the tribunes were the guardians of the rights of the plebeians) 286
promised forth previously engaged 288 *hold* change not 293 *quick
mettle* of a lively temperament 296 *tardy form* sluggish pose 297 *wit*
intellect 298 *stomach* appetite, disposition; *disgest* digest 302 *come home
to* visit

Come home to me, and I will wait for you.

CASSIUS

304   I will do so. Till then, think of the world.   *Exit Brutus.*
   Well, Brutus, thou art noble ; yet I see
306   Thy honorable mettle may be wrought
   From that it is disposed. Therefore it is meet
   That noble minds keep ever with their likes ;
   For who so firm that cannot be seduced ?
310   Caesar doth bear me hard ; but he loves Brutus.
   If I were Brutus now and he were Cassius,
312   He should not humor me. I will this night,
313   In several hands, in at his windows throw,
   As if they came from several citizens,
315   Writings, all tending to the great opinion
   That Rome holds of his name ; wherein obscurely
317   Caesar's ambition shall be glancèd at.
318   And after this let Caesar seat him sure,
319   For we will shake him, or worse days endure.   *Exit.*

*

I, iii   *Thunder and lightning. Enter, [from opposite sides,]*
       Casca, [with his sword drawn,] and Cicero.

CICERO

1   Good even, Casca. Brought you Caesar home ?
   Why are you breathless ? and why stare you so ?

CASCA

3   Are not you moved when all the sway of earth
   Shakes like a thing unfirm ? O Cicero,
   I have seen tempests when the scolding winds

---

304 *the world* i.e. the times we are experiencing   306–07 *wrought . . . disposed* so worked upon as to change its natural qualities   310 *bear me hard* bear a grudge against me   312 *He* i.e. Brutus; *humor* persuade by flattery   313 *several hands* different handwritings   315 *tending . . . opinion* concerning the high respect   317 *glancèd* hinted   318 *him sure* himself firmly in power   319 *shake him* i.e. from his dominant position
I, iii A street   1 *Brought* accompanied, escorted   3 *sway* established order

Have rived the knotty oaks, and I have seen   6
Th' ambitious ocean swell and rage and foam
To be exalted with the threat'ning clouds;   8
But never till to-night, never till now,
Did I go through a tempest dropping fire.
Either there is a civil strife in heaven,
Or else the world, too saucy with the gods,   12
Incenses them to send destruction.

CICERO
Why, saw you any thing more wonderful?

CASCA
A common slave (you know him well by sight)·
Held up his left hand, which did flame and burn
Like twenty torches joined; and yet his hand,
Not sensible of fire, remained unscorched.   18
Besides (I ha' not since put up my sword),
Against the Capitol I met a lion,   20
Who glazed upon me, and went surly by   21
Without annoying me. And there were drawn   22
Upon a heap a hundred ghastly women,   23
Transformèd with their fear, who swore they saw
Men, all in fire, walk up and down the streets.
And yesterday the bird of night did sit   26
Even at noonday upon the market place,
Hooting and shrieking. When these prodigies   28
Do so conjointly meet, let not men say
'These are their reasons – they are natural,'
For I believe they are portentous things
Unto the climate that they point upon.   32

CICERO
Indeed it is a strange-disposèd time.
But men may construe things after their fashion,   34

6 *rived* split   8 *exalted with* raised to the level of   12 *saucy* insolent   18
sensible of feeling   20 *Against* opposite   21 *glazed* stared   22–23 *drawn* ...
heap crowded together   23 *ghastly* pale as ghosts   26 *bird of night* screech
owl (proverbially ill-omened)   28 *prodigies* monstrous events   32 *climate*
region   34 *construe* (cf. I, ii, 45n.); *after their fashion* each in his own way

35   Clean from the purpose of the things themselves.
        Comes Caesar to the Capitol to-morrow?

CASCA

He doth; for he did bid Antonius
Send word to you he would be there to-morrow.

CICERO

Good night then, Casca. This disturbèd sky
Is not to walk in.

CASCA   Farewell, Cicero.   *Exit Cicero.*
                Enter Cassius.

CASSIUS

Who's there?

CASCA   A Roman.

CASSIUS   Casca, by your voice.

CASCA

Your ear is good. Cassius, what night is this?

CASSIUS

A very pleasing night to honest men.

CASCA

Who ever knew the heavens menace so?

CASSIUS

Those that have known the earth so full of faults.
For my part, I have walked about the streets,
Submitting me unto the perilous night,

48   And, thus unbracèd, Casca, as you see,
49   Have bared my bosom to the thunder-stone;
50   And when the cross blue lightning seemed to open
        The breast of heaven, I did present myself
        Even in the aim and very flash of it.

CASCA

But wherefore did you so much tempt the heavens?

54   It is the part of men to fear and tremble
        When the most mighty gods by tokens send

56   Such dreadful heralds to astonish us.

---

35 *Clean . . . purpose* contrary to the meaning   48 *unbracèd* with doublet un-
buttoned, i.e. exposed   49 *thunder-stone* thunderbolt, lightning   50 *cross*
forked   54 *part* appropriate action   56 *heralds* precursors; *astonish* terrify

CASSIUS

You are dull, Casca, and those sparks of life
That should be in a Roman you do want,   58
Or else you use not. You look pale, and gaze,
And put on fear, and cast yourself in wonder;   60
To see the strange impatience of the heavens;
But if you would consider the true cause –
Why all these fires, why all these gliding ghosts,
Why birds and beasts, from quality and kind;   64
Why old men, fools, and children calculate;   65
Why all these things change from their ordinance,   66
Their natures, and preformèd faculties,   67
To monstrous quality – why, you shall find   68
That heaven hath infused them with these spirits   69
To make them instruments of fear and warning
Unto some monstrous state.
Now could I, Casca, name to thee a man
Most like this dreadful night
That thunders, lightens, opens graves, and roars
As doth the lion in the Capitol;
A man no mightier than thyself or me
In personal action, yet prodigious grown
And fearful, as these strange eruptions are.   78

CASCA

'Tis Caesar that you mean. Is it not, Cassius?

CASSIUS

Let it be who it is. For Romans now
Have thews and limbs like to their ancestors;
But woe the while, our fathers' minds are dead,   82
And we are governed with our mothers' spirits;

58 *want* lack   **60** *put on* manifest; *cast . . . wonder* are astonished   **64** *from
. . . kind* contrary to their nature (in behavior)   **65** *old men* i.e. in their second
childhood; *calculate* compute future events (proverbially children and fools
speak truth, without discourse of reason)   **66** *ordinance* established modes
of behavior   **67** *preformèd faculties* congenital qualities   **68** *monstrous* unnatural   **69** *spirits* powers (?), demons (?)   **78** *fearful* causing fear; *eruptions* disturbances of natural and accustomed order   **82** *woe the while* alas for
the times

84   Our yoke and sufferance show us womanish.

CASCA

Indeed, they say the senators to-morrow
Mean to establish Caesar as a king,
And he shall wear his crown by sea and land
88   In every place save here in Italy.

CASSIUS

I know where I will wear this dagger then;
Cassius from bondage will deliver Cassius.
91   Therein, ye gods, you make the weak most strong;
Therein, ye gods, you tyrants do defeat.
Nor stony tower, nor walls of beaten brass,
Nor airless dungeon, nor strong links of iron,
95   Can be retentive to the strength of spirit;
But life, being weary of these worldly bars,
Never lacks power to dismiss itself.
98   If I know this, know all the world besides,
That part of tyranny that I do bear
100   I can shake off at pleasure.
                Thunder still.

CASCA   So can I.
So every bondman in his own hand bears
The power to cancel his captivity.

CASSIUS

And why should Caesar be a tyrant then?
Poor man! I know he would not be a wolf
But that he sees the Romans are but sheep;
106   He were no lion, were not Romans hinds.
Those that with haste will make a mighty fire
Begin it with weak straws. What trash is Rome,
What rubbish and what offal, when it serves
For the base matter to illuminate
So vile a thing as Caesar! But, O grief,

84 *yoke and sufferance* i.e. meek endurance of tyranny   88 *every place* all
parts of the Roman Empire   91 *Therein* i.e. in suicide   95 *be retentive to*
confine   98 *know all . . . besides* let everyone else know   100 s.d. *still*
continually   106 *hinds* does (with pun on 'peasants')

Where hast thou led me? I, perhaps, speak this
Before a willing bondman. Then I know
My answer must be made. But I am armed,
And dangers are to me indifferent.   115

CASCA
You speak to Casca, and to such a man
That is no fleering telltale. Hold, my hand.   117
Be factious for redress of all these griefs,   118
And I will set this foot of mine as far
As who goes farthest.
          [*They shake hands.*]
CASSIUS   There's a bargain made.
Now know you, Casca, I have moved already
Some certain of the noblest-minded Romans
To undergo with me an enterprise   123
Of honorable dangerous consequence;   124
And I do know, by this they stay for me   125
In Pompey's Porch; for now, this fearful night,   126
There is no stir or walking in the streets,
And the complexion of the element   128
Is fev'rous, like the work we have in hand,   129
Most bloody, fiery, and most terrible.
          Enter Cinna.

CASCA
Stand close awhile, for here comes one in haste.   131
CASSIUS
'Tis Cinna. I do know him by his gait.
He is a friend. Cinna, where haste you so?
CINNA
To find out you. Who's that? Metellus Cimber?   134

---

115 *indifferent* a matter of indifference   117 *fleering* mocking, flattering
118 *factious* politically active   123 *undergo* undertake   124 *honorable*
honorably   125 *by . . . stay* by this time they are waiting   126 *Pompey's
Porch* the colonnade of the great theatre built by Pompey   128 *complexion
. . . element* appearance of the sky   129 *fev'rous* feverish (the folio 'Fauors'
is sometimes otherwise emended to 'favored,' i.e. featured)   131 *close*
concealed   134 *find out* look for

CASSIUS

135   No, it is Casca, one incorporate
       To our attempts. Am I not stayed for, Cinna?

CINNA

137   I am glad on't. What a fearful night is this!
       There's two or three of us have seen strange sights.

CASSIUS

       Am I not stayed for? Tell me.

CINNA   Yes, you are.
       O Cassius, if you could
       But win the noble Brutus to our party –

CASSIUS

       Be you content. Good Cinna, take this paper
143   And look you lay it in the praetor's chair,
       Where Brutus may but find it. And throw this
       In at his window. Set this up with wax
146   Upon old Brutus' statue. All this done,
       Repair to Pompey's Porch, where you shall find us.
148   Is Decius Brutus and Trebonius there?

CINNA

       All but Metellus Cimber, and he's gone
150   To seek you at your house. Well, I will hie
151   And so bestow these papers as you bade me.

CASSIUS

152   That done, repair to Pompey's Theatre.   *Exit Cinna.*
153   Come, Casca, you and I will yet ere day
154   See Brutus at his house. Three parts of him
       Is ours already, and the man entire
156   Upon the next encounter yields him ours.

CASCA

       O, he sits high in all the people's hearts;

135 *incorporate* closely associated   137 *on't* of it   143 *praetor's chair*
official seat of the highest judicial magistrate, at that time Brutus (see II,
iv, 35n.)   146 *old Brutus' statue* (see I, ii, 159n.)   148 *Decius Brutus* a
kinsman of Marcus Brutus; his name was really Decimus   150 *hie* hasten
151 *bestow* distribute   152 *repair* return   153 *ere* before   154 *Three parts*
three-quarters (?), three of the four humours in man (?) (see V, v, 73n.)
156 *yields him ours* i.e. will join our faction

48

And that which would appear offense in us,
His countenance, like richest alchemy,   159
Will change to virtue and to worthiness.

CASSIUS
Him and his worth and our great need of him
You have right well conceited. Let us go,   162
For it is after midnight; and ere day
We will awake him and be sure of him.   *Exeunt.*

*

Enter Brutus in his orchard.   II, i

BRUTUS
What, Lucius, ho!
I cannot by the progress of the stars
Give guess how near to day. Lucius, I say!
I would it were my fault to sleep so soundly.
When, Lucius, when? Awake, I say! What, Lucius!   5
          Enter Lucius.

LUCIUS Called you, my lord?

BRUTUS
Get me a taper in my study, Lucius.
When it is lighted, come and call me here.

LUCIUS I will, my lord.   *Exit.*

BRUTUS
It must be by his death, and for my part,
I know no personal cause to spurn at him,   11
But for the general. He would be crowned.   12
How that might change his nature, there's the question.
It is the bright day that brings forth the adder,
And that craves wary walking. Crown him that,   15

---

159 *countenance* support; *alchemy* the proto-science devoted to transmuting
base metals into gold   **162** *conceited* conceived (with pun on 'expressed in a
fanciful simile')
II, i By the house of Brutus   **s.d.** *orchard* garden   **5** *When* (exclamation
of impatience)   **11** *spurn at* kick against   **12** *general* public welfare, health
of the state   **15** *craves* calls for; *Crown him that* i.e. king (a word Brutus here
avoids)

And then I grant we put a sting in him
17　That at his will he may do danger with.
Th' abuse of greatness is, when it disjoins
19　Remorse from power. And to speak truth of Caesar,
20　I have not known when his affections swayed
21　More than his reason. But 'tis a common proof
22　That lowliness is young ambition's ladder,
Whereto the climber upward turns his face;
But when he once attains the upmost round,
He then unto the ladder turns his back,
26　Looks in the clouds, scorning the base degrees
By which he did ascend. So Caesar may.
28　Then lest he may, prevent. And since the quarrel
29　Will bear no color for the thing he is,
30　Fashion it thus: that what he is, augmented,
31　Would run to these and these extremities;
And therefore think him as a serpent's egg,
33　Which, hatched, would as his kind grow mischievous,
And kill him in the shell.
　　　　Enter Lucius.

LUCIUS
35　The taper burneth in your closet, sir.
Searching the window for a flint, I found
This paper, thus sealed up; and I am sure
It did not lie there when I went to bed.
　　　　Gives him the letter.

BRUTUS
Get you to bed again; it is not day.
Is not to-morrow, boy, the ides of March?

---

17 *danger* harm　**19** *Remorse* mercy　**20** *affections swayed* passions ruled
21 *common proof* commonplace, conventional observation based on experience　**22** *lowliness* apparent humility　**26** *base degrees* lower rungs
of the ladder (with pun on 'lower grades of office,' possibly referring to
the Roman *'cursus honorum'*)　**28** *prevent* take measures to forestall;
quarrel case (against Caesar)　**29** *bear no color* carry no conviction　**30**
Fashion it put the case　**31** *extremities* extremes (of tyranny)　**33** *his kind*
its nature is　**35** *closet* study

LUCIUS I know not, sir.

BRUTUS

    Look in the calendar and bring me word.   42

LUCIUS I will, sir.   *Exit.*

BRUTUS

    The exhalations, whizzing in the air,   44
    Give so much light that I may read by them.
        Opens the letter and reads.
     'Brutus, thou sleep'st. Awake, and see thyself!
      Shall Rome, &c. Speak, strike, redress!'   47
    'Brutus, thou sleep'st. Awake!'
    Such instigations have been often dropped
    Where I have took them up.
    'Shall Rome, &c.' Thus must I piece it out: 51
    Shall Rome stand under one man's awe? What, Rome?   52
    My ancestors did from the streets of Rome   53
    The Tarquin drive when he was called a king.
    'Speak, strike, redress!' Am I entreated
    To speak and strike? O Rome, I make thee promise,
    If the redress will follow, thou receivest   57
    Thy full petition at the hand of Brutus!   58
        Enter Lucius.

LUCIUS

    Sir, March is wasted fifteen days.   59
        Knock within.

BRUTUS

    'Tis good. Go to the gate; somebody knocks.
              [Exit Lucius.]
    Since Cassius first did whet me against Caesar,
    I have not slept.
    Between the acting of a dreadful thing

---

42 *calendar* (the Julian calendar, instituted by Caesar in 46 B.C.) 44
exhalations meteors 47, 51 *&c.* (read *'et cetera'*) 52 *under . . . awe* in fear
of one man 53 *ancestors* (see I, ii, 159n.) 57 *redress* i.e. correction of
abuses in the Republic 58 *Thy full petition* all you ask 59 *fifteen* (the
Romans counted both the day from which and the day to which they
reckoned)

64 And the first motion, all the interim is
65 Like a phantasma or a hideous dream.
66 The genius and the mortal instruments
67 Are then in council, and the state of a man,
    Like to a little kingdom, suffers then
    The nature of an insurrection.
                Enter Lucius.
LUCIUS
70 Sir, 'tis your brother Cassius at the door,
    Who doth desire to see you.
BRUTUS   Is he alone?
LUCIUS
72 No, sir, there are moe with him.
BRUTUS   Do you know them?
LUCIUS
    No, sir. Their hats are plucked about their ears
    And half their faces buried in their cloaks,
75 That by no means I may discover them
76 By any mark of favor.
BRUTUS   Let 'em enter.   *[Exit Lucius.]*
    They are the faction. O conspiracy,
    Sham'st thou to show thy dang'rous brow by night,
79 When evils are most free? O, then by day
    Where wilt thou find a cavern dark enough
    To mask thy monstrous visage? Seek none, conspiracy.
    Hide it in smiles and affability:
83 For if thou path, thy native semblance on,
84 Not Erebus itself were dim enough
85 To hide thee from prevention.

64 *motion* proposal 65 *phantasma* hallucination, nightmare 66 *genius* guardian spirit; *mortal instruments* intellectual and emotional faculties 67 *in council* deliberating; *of a man* (many editors delete 'a') 70 *brother* i.e. brother-in-law (Cassius was married to Brutus' sister, Junia) 72 *moe* more 75 *discover* recognize, identify 76 *favor* appearance 79 *evils . . . free* evil things range abroad most freely 83 *path* walk; *native semblance* true form 84 *Erebus* region of primeval darkness between the upper Earth and Hades 85 *prevention* being forestalled

Enter the Conspirators, Cassius, Casca, Decius,
Cinna, Metellus [Cimber], and Trebonius.

CASSIUS
    I think we are too bold upon your rest.   86
    Good morrow, Brutus. Do we trouble you?

BRUTUS
    I have been up this hour, awake all night.
    Know I these men that come along with you?

CASSIUS
    Yes, every man of them; and no man here
    But honors you; and every one doth wish   *FLATTERY*
    You had but that opinion of yourself
    Which every noble Roman bears of you.
    This is Trebonius.

BRUTUS   He is welcome hither.

CASSIUS
    This, Decius Brutus.

BRUTUS   He is welcome too.

CASSIUS
    This, Casca; this, Cinna; and this, Metellus Cimber.

BRUTUS
    They are all welcome.
    What watchful cares do interpose themselves   98
    Betwixt your eyes and night?

CASSIUS
    Shall I entreat a word?
        They whisper.

DECIUS
    Here lies the east. Doth not the day break here?

CASCA No.

CINNA
    O, pardon, sir, it doth; and yon grey lines
    That fret the clouds are messengers of day.   104

CASCA
    You shall confess that you are both deceived.

86 *upon* in intruding on   98 *watchful cares* concerns that keep you awake
104 *fret* ornamentally interlace

Here, as I point my sword, the sun arises,
107   Which is a great way growing on the south,
108   Weighing the youthful season of the year.
Some two months hence, up higher toward the north
110   He first presents his fire ; and the high east
Stands as the Capitol, directly here.

BRUTUS
Give me your hands all over, one by one.

CASSIUS
And let us swear our resolution.

BRUTUS   1st DISAGREEMENT
114   No, not an oath. If not the face of men,
115   The sufferance of our souls, the time's abuse –
116   If these be motives weak, break off betimes,
117   And every man hence to his idle bed.
118   So let high-sighted tyranny range on
119   Till each man drop by lottery. But if these
120   (As I am sure they do) bear fire enough
To kindle cowards and to steel with valor
122   The melting spirits of women, then, countrymen,
123   What need we any spur but our own cause
124   To prick us to redress ? what other bond
125   Than secret Romans that have spoke the word
126   And will not palter ? and what other oath
127   Than honesty to honesty engaged
That this shall be, or we will fall for it ?

107 *growing on* toward   108 *Weighing* considering   110 *high* due, exact
114 *face* appearance (which should be identical with reality), i.e. the serious
manner of the conspirators and the anxious manner of their fellow citizens
115 *sufferance* distress; *time's abuse* corruption of these days (i.e. Caesar's
violation of the laws of the Republic)   116 *betimes* at once   117 *idle* unused
118 *high-sighted* looking down from on high (like a falcon), i.e. arrogant
119 *lottery* whim   120 *fire* i.e. spirit, courage   122 *melting* yielding   123
What why   124 *prick* spur   125 *secret Romans* the mere fact that we are
Romans able to hold our tongues (?), sharing a secret (?); *spoke the word*
given one another our word of honor   126 *palter* quibble   127 *honesty*
personal honor; *engaged* pledged

Swear priests and cowards and men cautelous,   129
Old feeble carrions and such suffering souls   130
That welcome wrongs ; unto bad causes swear
Such creatures as men doubt ; but do not stain
The even virtue of our enterprise,   133
Nor th' insuppressive mettle of our spirits,   134
To think that or our cause or our performance   135
Did need an oath ; when every drop of blood
That every Roman bears, and nobly bears,
Is guilty of a several bastardy   138
If he do break the smallest particle
Of any promise that hath passed from him.

CASSIUS
　　But what of Cicero ? Shall we sound him ?   141
　　I think he will stand very strong with us.

CASCA
　　Let us not leave him out.
CINNA　　　　　　　　　　No, by no means.
METELLUS
　　O, let us have him, for his silver hairs
　　Will purchase us a good opinion   145
　　And buy men's voices to commend our deeds.
　　It shall be said his judgment ruled our hands.
　　Our youths and wildness shall no whit appear,   148
　　But all be buried in his gravity.   149
BRUTUS
　　O, name him not. Let us not break with him ;   150
　　For he will never follow anything
　　That other men begin.
CASSIUS　　　　　　　　Then leave him out.
CASCA
　　Indeed he is not fit.

129 *Swear* make swear, bind by oath; *cautelous* crafty, deceitful 130
carrions physical wrecks, practically corpses 133 *even* uniform, un-
blemished 134 *insuppressive* indomitable; *mettle* (see I, i, 61n.) 135 *or ...*
or either ... or 138 *several* separate, individual 141 *sound* feel out 145
purchase procure; *opinion* reputation 148 *no whit* not at all 149 *gravity*
sobriety and authority of character 150 *break with* put the matter to

55

DECIUS
        Shall no man else be touched but only Caesar?
CASSIUS
155   Decius, well urged. I think it is not meet
        Mark Antony, so well beloved of Caesar,
157   Should outlive Caesar. We shall find of him
158   A shrewd contriver; and you know, his means,
159   If he improve them, may well stretch so far
160   As to annoy us all; which to prevent,
        Let Antony and Caesar fall together.
BRUTUS
        Our course will seem too bloody, Caius Cassius,
        To cut the head off and then hack the limbs,
164   Like wrath in death and envy afterwards;
165   For Antony is but a limb of Caesar.
        Let's be sacrificers, but not butchers, Caius.
167   We all stand up against the spirit of Caesar,
        And in the spirit of men there is no blood.
169   O that we then could come by Caesar's spirit
        And not dismember Caesar! But, alas,
171   Caesar must bleed for it. And, gentle friends,
        Let's kill him boldly, but not wrathfully;
        Let's carve him as a dish fit for the gods,
        Not hew him as a carcass fit for hounds.
175   And let our hearts, as subtle masters do,
        Stir up their servants to an act of rage
        And after seem to chide 'em. This shall make
178   Our purpose necessary, and not envious;
        Which so appearing to the common eyes,
180   We shall be called purgers, not murderers.
        And for Mark Antony, think not of him;

155 *urged* recommended   157 *of* in   158 *shrewd contriver* formidable
plotter; *means* capacity (to harm us)   159 *improve* exploit   160 *annoy*
injure; *prevent* forestall   164 *envy* malice   165 *limb* mere appendage
167 *spirit* principles (i.e. Caesarism)   169 *come by* get at   171 *gentle* noble
175–77 *And . . . chide 'em* i.e. let us not be wrathful in our hearts although
our hands must be made to perform this violent act (in order to preserve
the Republic)   178 *envious* malicious   180 *purgers* healers

For he can do no more than Caesar's arm
When Caesar's head is off.

CASSIUS   Yet I fear him;
For in the ingrafted love he bears to Caesar –   184

BRUTUS

Alas, good Cassius, do not think of him!
If he love Caesar, all that he can do
Is to himself – take thought, and die for Caesar.   187
And that were much he should; for he is given   188
To sports, to wildness, and much company.

TREBONIUS

There is no fear in him. Let him not die;   190
For he will live, and laugh at this hereafter.
        Clock strikes.

BRUTUS

Peace! Count the clock.

CASSIUS   The clock hath stricken three.

TREBONIUS

'Tis time to part.

CASSIUS   But it is doubtful yet
Whether Caesar will come forth to-day or no;   194
For he is superstitious grown of late,
Quite from the main opinion he held once   196
Of fantasy, of dreams, and ceremonies.   197
It may be these apparent prodigies,   198
The unaccustomed terror of this night,
And the persuasion of his augurers   200
May hold him from the Capitol to-day.

DECIUS

Never fear that. If he be so resolved,
I can o'ersway him; for he loves to hear   203

184 *ingrafted* deeply implanted 187 *take thought* fall into a melancholy
state 188 *that...should* it is unlikely that he would 190 *no fear* nothing to
fear 194 *Whether* (pronounced, and often spelled, 'where' or 'whe'r')
196 *from the main* contrary to the strong 197 *fantasy* fancy, i.e. imaginary
fears; *ceremonies* portents 198 *apparent prodigies* manifest signs of disaster
200 *augurers* augurs (priests who interpreted omens) 203 *o'ersway*
persuade

204 That unicorns may be betrayed with trees
205 And bears with glasses, elephants with holes,
206 Lions with toils, and men with flatterers;
     But when I tell him he hates flatterers,
     He says he does, being then most flatterèd.
     Let me work;
210 For I can give his humor the true bent
     And I will bring him to the Capitol.

CASSIUS
212 Nay, we will all of us be there to fetch him.

BRUTUS
213 By the eight hour. Is that the uttermost?

CINNA
     Be that the uttermost, and fail not then.

METELLUS
215 Caius Ligarius doth bear Caesar hard,
216 Who rated him for speaking well of Pompey.
     I wonder none of you have thought of him.

BRUTUS
218 Now, good Metellus, go along by him.
     He loves me well, and I have given him reasons.
220 Send him but hither, and I'll fashion him.

CASSIUS
     The morning comes upon's. We'll leave you, Brutus.
     And, friends, disperse yourselves; but all remember
     What you have said and show yourselves true Romans.

BRUTUS
224 Good gentlemen, look fresh and merrily.
225 Let not our looks put on our purposes,
226 But bear it as our Roman actors do,
227 With untired spirits and formal constancy.

---

204 *betrayed with trees* tricked into running their horns into tree trunks, thence easily captured **205** *glasses* mirrors; *holes* pits **206** *toils* snares **210** *humor* disposition; *bent* direction **212** *fetch* escort **213** *eight* eighth; *uttermost* latest **215** *bear Caesar hard* (see I, ii, 310n.) **216** *rated* upbraided **218** *him* his house **220** *fashion* shape (to our purposes) **224** *fresh* brightly **225** *put on* display **226** *bear it* play your roles **227** *untired* alert; *formal constancy* proper self-possession

And so good morrow to you every one.
                              Exeunt. Manet Brutus.
Boy! Lucius! Fast asleep? It is no matter.
Enjoy the honey-heavy dew of slumber.   230
Thou hast no figures nor no fantasies   231
Which busy care draws in the brains of men;
Therefore thou sleep'st so sound.
        Enter Portia.
PORTIA   Brutus, my lord.
BRUTUS
Portia! What mean you? Wherefore rise you now?
It is not for your health thus to commit   235
Your weak condition to the raw cold morning.
PORTIA
Nor for yours neither. Y' have ungently, Brutus,   237
Stole from my bed. And yesternight at supper
You suddenly arose and walked about,
Musing and sighing with your arms across;   240
And when I asked you what the matter was,
You stared upon me with ungentle looks.
I urged you further; then you scratched your head
And too impatiently stamped with your foot.
Yet I insisted; yet you answered not,
But with an angry wafter of your hand   246
Gave sign for me to leave you. So I did,
Fearing to strengthen that impatience
Which seemed too much enkindled, and withal
Hoping it was but an effect of humor,   250
Which sometime hath his hour with every man.   251
It will not let you eat not talk nor sleep,
And could it work so much upon your shape
As it hath much prevailed on your condition,   254

---

230 *honey-heavy dew* i.e. sweetly drowsy refreshment   **231** *figures* figments
of imagination   **235** *commit* expose   **237** *ungently* ignobly, discourteously
240 *across* folded across your chest (a sign of melancholy)   **246** *wafter*
wafture, gesture   **250** *effect of humor* symptom of a temporary mood   **251**
his its   **254** *condition* disposition

255   I should not know you Brutus. Dear my lord,
       Make me acquainted with your cause of grief.

BRUTUS
       I am not well in health, and that is all.

PORTIA
       Brutus is wise and, were he not in health,
259   He would embrace the means to come by it.

BRUTUS
       Why, so I do. Good Portia, go to bed.

PORTIA
261   Is Brutus sick, and is it physical
262   To walk unbracèd and suck up the humors
       Of the dank morning? What, is Brutus sick,
       And will he steal out of his wholesome bed
265   To dare the vile contagion of the night,
266   And tempt the rheumy and unpurgèd air,
       To add unto his sickness? No, my Brutus.
268   You have some sick offense within your mind,
269   Which by the right and virtue of my place
          [Kneels.]
       I ought to know of; and upon my knees
271   I charm you, by my once commended beauty,
       By all your vows of love, and that great vow
273   Which did incorporate and make us one,
274   That you unfold to me, your self, your half,
275   Why you are heavy – and what men to-night
       Have had resort to you; for here have been
       Some six or seven, who did hide their faces
       Even from darkness.

BRUTUS   Kneel not, gentle Portia.
       [Raises her.]

---

255 *know you* recognize you as   **259** *embrace* adopt; *come by* regain   **261** *physical* healthful   **262** *unbracèd* (see I, iii, 48n.); *humors* mists, dews   **265** *vile . . . night* (night air was thought to be poisonous)   **266** *tempt* risk; *rheumy* moist; *unpurgèd* not purified (by the sun)   **268** *sick offense* harmful illness   **269** *virtue* power; *place* (as your wife)   **271** *charm* solemnly entreat   **273** *incorporate* make us one flesh   **274** *unfold* disclose; *self* other self; *half* i.e. wife   **275** *heavy* sad

PORTIA

    I should not need if you were gentle Brutus.
    Within the bond of marriage, tell me, Brutus,
    Is it excepted I should know no secrets   281
    That appertain to you? Am I your self
    But, as it were, in sort or limitation?   283
    To keep with you at meals, comfort your bed,   284
    And talk to you sometimes? Dwell I but in the suburbs   285
    Of your good pleasure? If it be no more,
    Portia is Brutus' harlot, not his wife.

BRUTUS

    You are my true and honorable wife,
    As dear to me as are the ruddy drops
    That visit my sad heart.

PORTIA

    If this were true, then should I know this secret.
    I grant I am a woman; but withal
    A woman that Lord Brutus took to wife.
    I grant I am a woman; but withal
    A woman well-reputed, Cato's daughter.   295
    Think you I am no stronger than my sex,
    Being so fathered and so husbanded?
    Tell me your counsels; I will not disclose 'em.   298
    I have made strong proof of my constancy,   299
    Giving myself a voluntary wound
    Here, in the thigh. Can I bear that with patience,
    And not my husband's secrets?

BRUTUS   O ye gods,

    Render me worthy of this noble wife!

        Knock.

    Hark, hark! One knocks. Portia, go in awhile,

281 *excepted* made an exception that   283 *in . . . limitation* after a fashion or under restriction (a legalism)   284 *keep* keep company   285 *suburbs* outlying districts (notorious for their brothels and other disreputable haunts)   295 *Cato* (Cato of Utica, famous for absolute moral integrity, fought with Pompey against Caesar and killed himself to avoid capture in 46 B.C.; he was Brutus' uncle as well as father-in-law)   298 *counsels* secrets   299 *proof* trial; *constancy* fortitude

HE WILL TELL HER LATER

And by and by thy bosom shall partake
The secrets of my heart.

307 All my engagements I will construe to thee,
308 All the charactery of my sad brows.
Leave me with haste.   *Exit Portia.*
                    Lucius, who's that knocks?
Enter Lucius and [Caius] Ligarius.

LUCIUS
Here is a sick man that would speak with you.

BRUTUS
Caius Ligarius, that Metellus spake of.
312 Boy, stand aside. Caius Ligarius, how?

CAIUS
313 Vouchsafe good morrow from a feeble tongue.

BRUTUS
314 O, what a time have you chose out, brave Caius,
315 To wear a kerchief! Would you were not sick.

CAIUS
I am not sick if Brutus have in hand
Any exploit worthy the name of honor.

BRUTUS
Such an exploit have I in hand, Ligarius,
Had you a healthful ear to hear of it.

CAIUS
By all the gods that Romans bow before,
I here discard my sickness.
          [Throws off his kerchief.]   Soul of Rome,
322 Brave son derived from honorable loins,
323 Thou like an exorcist hast conjured up
324 My mortified spirit. Now bid me run,
And I will strive with things impossible;
Yea, get the better of them. What's to do?

---

307 *engagements* commitments; *construe* explain fully   **308** *the charactery of* that which is written in shorthand upon (accent 'charàctery')   **312** *how* how are you   **313** *Vouchsafe* deign to accept   **314** *brave* noble   **315** *To . . . kerchief* i.e. to be sick   **322** *derived . . . loins* (see I, ii, 159n.)   **323** *exorcist* conjurer   **324** *mortified* deadened, as if dead

BRUTUS

A piece of work that will make sick men whole. 327

CAIUS

But are not some whole that we must make sick? 328

BRUTUS

That must we also. What it is, my Caius,
I shall unfold to thee as we are going 330
To whom it must be done. 331

CAIUS   Set on your foot,
And with a heart new-fired I follow you,
To do I know not what; but it sufficeth
That Brutus leads me on.
        Thunder.

BRUTUS   Follow me then.   *Exeunt.*

*

Thunder and lightning. Enter Julius Caesar, in his   II, ii
nightgown.

CAESAR

Nor heaven nor eath have been at peace to-night. 1
Thrice hath Calphurnia in her sleep cried out
'Help, ho! They murder Caesar!' Who's within? 3
        Enter a Servant.

SERVANT My lord?

CAESAR

Go bid the priests do present sacrifice, 5
And bring me their opinions of success. 6

SERVANT I will, my lord.   *Exit.*
        Enter Calphurnia.

CALPHURNIA

What mean you, Caesar? Think you to walk forth?

---

327 *whole* healthy   328 *make sick* i.e. kill   330 *unfold* disclose   331 *To whom* to the house of him to whom; *Set on* advance
II, ii Within the house of Caesar   s.d. *nightgown* dressing gown   1 *Nor . . . nor* neither . . . nor   3 *Who's within* which of the servants is about   5 *priests* augurs (see II, i, 200n.); *present* immediate   6 *opinions of success* judgments of the success or failure of my plans

You shall not stir out of your house to-day.

CAESAR

[handwritten: HE IS MIGATIER THAN FEAR]

Caesar shall forth. The things that threatened me
Ne'er looked but on my back. When they shall see
The face of Caesar, they are vanishèd.

CALPHURNIA

13   Caesar, I never stood on ceremonies,
Yet now they fright me. There is one within,
Besides the things that we have heard and seen,

16   Recounts most horrid sights seen by the watch.
A lioness hath whelpèd in the streets,
And graves have yawned and yielded up their dead.
Fierce fiery warriors fought upon the clouds

20   In ranks and squadrons and right form of war,
Which drizzled blood upon the Capitol.

22   The noise of battle hurtled in the air,
Horses did neigh, and dying men did groan,
And ghosts did shriek and squeal about the streets.

25   O Caesar, these things are beyond all use,
And I do fear them.

CAESAR   What can be avoided
Whose end is purposed by the mighty gods?
[handwritten check mark] Yet Caesar shall go forth; for these predictions

29   Are to the world in general as to Caesar.

CALPHURNIA   *[handwritten: CAESAR = DANGER]*

[handwritten check mark] When beggars die there are no comets seen;

31   The heavens themselves blaze forth the death of princes.

CAESAR   *[handwritten: SUFFER]*

Cowards die many times before their deaths;
The valiant never taste of death but once.
Of all the wonders that I yet have heard,
It seems to me most strange that men should fear,
Seeing that death, a necessary end,

---

13 *stood on ceremonies* heeded portents 16 *watch* nightwatchmen 20
right form regular order 22 *hurtled* clashed 25 *use* normal experience
29 *Are to* are as applicable to 31 *blaze forth* i.e. proclaim

Will come when it will come.
    Enter a Servant.   What say the augurers?

SERVANT
They would not have you to stir forth to-day.
Plucking the entrails of an offering forth,
They could not find a heart within the beast.

CAESAR
The gods do this in shame of cowardice.
Caesar should be a beast without a heart
If he should stay at home to-day for fear.   42
No, Caesar shall not. Danger knows full well
That Caesar is more dangerous than he.
We are two lions littered in one day,
And I the elder and more terrible,
And Caesar shall go forth.

CALPHURNIA   Alas, my lord,
Your wisdom is consumed in confidence!   49
Do not go forth to-day! Call it my fear
That keeps you in the house and not your own.
We'll send Mark Antony to the Senate House,
And he shall say you are not well to-day.
Let me upon my knee prevail in this.

CAESAR
Mark Antony shall say I am not well,
And for thy humor I will stay at home.   56
    Enter Decius.
Here's Decius Brutus; he shall tell them so.

DECIUS
Caesar, all hail! Good morrow, worthy Caesar;
I come to fetch you to the Senate House.   59

CAESAR
And you are come in very happy time   60
To bear my greeting to the senators
And tell them that I will not come to-day.

---

42 *should* would indeed   49 *consumed in confidence* destroyed by over-confidence   56 *humor* whim   59 *fetch* escort   60 *in . . . time* at a most opportune moment

Cannot, is false; and that I dare not, falser:
I will not come to-day. Tell them so, Decius.

CALPHURNIA
Say he is sick.

CAESAR   Shall Caesar send a lie?
Have I in conquest stretched mine arm so far
To be afeard to tell greybeards the truth!
Decius, go tell them Caesar will not come.

DECIUS
EMBARRASING
Most mighty Caesar, let me know some cause,
Lest I be laughed at when I tell them so.

CAESAR
The cause is in my will: I will not come.
That is enough to satisfy the Senate;
But for your private satisfaction,
Because I love you, I will let you know.

75   Calphurnia here, my wife, stays me at home.
76   She dreamt to-night she saw my statue,
      Which, like a fountain with an hundred spouts,
78   Did run pure blood; and many lusty Romans
      Came smiling and did bathe their hands in it.
80   And these does she apply for warnings and portents
      And evil imminent, and on her knee
      Hath begged that I will stay at home to-day.

DECIUS
This dream is all amiss interpreted;
It was a vision fair and fortunate.
Your statue spouting blood in many pipes,
In which so many smiling Romans bathed,
Signifies that from you great Rome shall suck
Reviving blood, and that great men shall press
89   For tinctures, stains, relics, and cognizance.
      This by Calphurnia's dream is signified.

75 _stays_ keeps · 76 _statue_ (trisyllabic) 78 _lusty_ vigorous, gallant 80
apply for interpret as; _portents_ (accent 'portènts') 89 _tinctures_ stains
(with heraldic and alchemical associations); _relics_ (as of holy martyrs);
cognizance an identifying emblem worn by a nobleman's followers

CAESAR
    And this way have you well expounded it.

DECIUS
    I have, when you have heard what I can say;
    And know it now. The Senate have concluded   93
    To give this day a crown to mighty Caesar.
    If you shall send them word you will not come,
    Their minds may change. Besides, it were a mock   96
    Apt to be rendered, for some one to say
    'Break up the Senate till another time,
    When Caesar's wife shall meet with better dreams.'
    If Caesar hide himself, shall they not whisper   100
    'Lo, Caesar is afraid'?
    Pardon me, Caesar; for my dear dear love
    To your proceeding bids me tell you this,   103
    And reason to my love is liable.   104

AMBITION PREVAILS

CAESAR
    How foolish do your fears seem now, Calphurnia!
    I am ashamèd I did yield to them.
    Give me my robe, for I will go.   107
        Enter Brutus, Ligarius, Metellus, Casca,
        Trebonius, Cinna, and Publius.
    And look where Publius is come to fetch me.

PUBLIUS
    Good morrow, Caesar.

CAESAR   Welcome, Publius.
    What, Brutus, are you stirred so early too?
    Good morrow, Casca. Caius Ligarius,
    Caesar was ne'er so much your enemy   112
    As that same ague which hath made you lean.   113
    What is't o'clock?

BRUTUS   Caesar, 'tis strucken eight.

93 *concluded* formally determined 96–97 *mock . . . rendered* sarcastic
remark likely to be made 100 *shall* will indeed 103 *proceeding* advance-
ment (?), career (?) 104 *reason . . . liable* i.e. my love outweighs my judgment in speaking thus freely to you 107 *robe* toga 112 *enemy* (Ligarius,
like Brutus, Cassius, and Cicero, had supported Pompey against Caesar)
113 *lean* (apparently the same actor took the parts of Cassius and Ligarius)

CAESAR
I thank you for your pains and courtesy.
        Enter Antony.
See, Antony, that revels long a-nights,
Is notwithstanding up. Good morrow, Antony.
ANTONY
118   So to most noble Caesar.
CAESAR   Bid them prepare within.
I am to blame to be thus waited for.
Now, Cinna. Now, Metellus. What, Trebonius;
I have an hour's talk in store for you;
Remember that you call on me to-day;   *IRONIC*
Be near me, that I may remember you.
TREBONIUS
124   Caesar, I will. *[aside]* And so near will I be
That your best friends shall wish I had been further.
CAESAR
Good friends, go in and taste some wine with me,
And we (like friends) will straightway go together.
BRUTUS *[aside]*
128   That every like is not the same, O Caesar,
129   The heart of Brutus erns to think upon.   *Exeunt.*

*

II, iii   *Enter Artemidorus [reading a paper].*
[ARTEMIDORUS] 'Caesar, beware of Brutus; take heed
of Cassius; come not near Casca; have an eye to Cinna;
trust not Trebonius; mark well Metellus Cimber;
Decius Brutus loves thee not; thou hast wronged Caius
Ligarius. There is but one mind in all these men, and it
6   is bent against Caesar. If thou beest not immortal, look

---

118 *So* likewise; *prepare* i.e. set out the wine   124–25 *And . . . further*
(actually Trebonius lures Antony out of the way before the assassination)
128 *every . . . same* i.e. appearance is not always the same as reality   129
erns grieves
II, iii A street near the Capitol   6 *bent* directed

about you. Security gives way to conspiracy. The 7
mighty gods defend thee!

                              'Thy lover,   9
                                    'Artemidorus.'

Here will I stand till Caesar pass along
And as a suitor will I give him this.   12
My heart laments that virtue cannot live
Out of the teeth of emulation.   14
If thou read this, O Caesar, thou mayest live;
If not, the Fates with traitors do contrive.   *Exit.* 16

How will he get this to Caesar?

*

        Enter Portia and Lucius.   II, iv
PORTIA
    I prithee, boy, run to the Senate House.
    Stay not to answer me, but get thee gone!
    Why dost thou stay?
LUCIUS   To know my errand, madam.
PORTIA
    I would have had thee there and here again
    Ere I can tell thee what thou shouldst do there.
        [*Aside*]
    O constancy, be strong upon my side,   6
    Set a huge mountain 'tween my heart and tongue!
    I have a man's mind, but a woman's might.   8
    How hard it is for women to keep counsel!   9
    Art thou here yet?
LUCIUS   Madam, what should I do?
    Run to the Capitol and nothing else?
    And so return to you and nothing else?

7 *Security* overconfidence; *way* path, opportunity 9 *lover* friend 12
as a suitor pretending to be a petitioner 14 *Out ... emulation* i.e. beyond
the reach of envious rivalry 16 *contrive* conspire
II, iv Before the house of Brutus 6 *constancy* self-control, fortitude
8 *might* strength 9 *counsel* a secret (i.e. Brutus' secret which he has told
her according to his promise; that he has had no opportunity to do so is
irrelevant by the Elizabethan theatrical convention of 'double time')

PORTIA
Yes, bring me word, boy, if thy lord look well,
14 For he went sickly forth; and take good note
What Caesar doth, what suitors press to him.
Hark, boy! What noise is that?

she's suspicious

LUCIUS
I hear none, madam.

PORTIA   Prithee listen well.
18 I heard a bustling rumor like a fray,
And the wind brings it from the Capitol.

LUCIUS
20 Sooth, madam, I hear nothing.
Enter the Soothsayer.

PORTIA
Come hither, fellow. Which way hast thou been?

SOOTHSAYER
At mine own house, good lady.

PORTIA
What is't o'clock?

SOOTHSAYER   About the ninth hour, lady.

PORTIA
Is Caesar yet gone to the Capitol?

SOOTHSAYER
Madam, not yet. I go to take my stand,
To see him pass on to the Capitol.

PORTIA
Thou hast some suit to Caesar, hast thou not?

SOOTHSAYER
That I have, lady, if it will please Caesar
To be so good to Caesar as to hear me:
I shall beseech him to befriend himself.

PORTIA
Why, know'st thou any harm's intended towards him?

---

14 *take good note* observe well   18 *bustling . . . fray* confused noise as in
battle   20 *Sooth* truly   s.d. *Soothsayer* (the same who had warned Caesar
at I, ii, 18)

SOOTHSAYER
  None that I know will be, much that I fear may chance.   32
  Good morrow to you. Here the street is narrow.
  The throng that follows Caesar at the heels,
  Of Senators, of praetors, common suitors,   35
  Will crowd a feeble man almost to death.
  I'll get me to a place more void and there   37
  Speak to great Caesar as he comes along.   *Exit.*

PORTIA
  I must go in. Ay me, how weak a thing
  The heart of woman is! O Brutus,
  The heavens speed thee in thine enterprise!
  Sure the boy heard me. – Brutus hath a suit
  That Caesar will not grant. – O, I grow faint. –
  Run, Lucius, and commend me to my lord;   44
  Say I am merry. Come to me again   45
  And bring me word what he doth say to thee.
                                   Exeunt [severally].

*

  Flourish. Enter Caesar, Brutus, Cassius, Casca,   III, i
  Decius, Metellus, Trebonius, Cinna, Antony,
  Lepidus, Artemidorus, [Popilius,] Publius, and the
  Soothsayer.

CAESAR
  The ides of March are come.

SOOTHSAYER
  Ay, Caesar, but not gone.

---

32 *chance* happen 35 *praetors* high-ranking judges in the administration
of Roman law (Caesar increased their number from eight to sixteen.
Brutus, Cassius, and Cinna were praetors in 44 B.C., Brutus being '*praetor
urbanus*,' the chief justice of the state and second only in authority to
the two consuls – Caesar, who had been appointed Dictator for life, and
Antony. Cassius, as '*praetor peregrinus*,' ranked immediately below
Brutus.) 37 *void* empty, spacious 44 *commend me* give my best love and
wishes 45 *merry* in good spirits
III, i Before the Capitol

ARTEMIDORUS
3   Hail, Caesar! Read this schedule.

DECIUS
Trebonius doth desire you to o'erread
(At your best leisure) this his humble suit.

ARTEMIDORUS
O Caesar, read mine first; for mine's a suit
7   That touches Caesar nearer. Read it, great Caesar!

CAESAR
8   What touches us ourself shall be last served.

ARTEMIDORUS
Delay not, Caesar! Read it instantly!

CAESAR
What, is the fellow mad?

10 PUBLIUS   Sirrah, give place.

CASSIUS
What, urge you your petitions in the street?
12 Come to the Capitol.
           [Caesar goes to the Capitol, the rest following.]

POPILIUS
13 I wish your enterprise to-day may thrive.

CASSIUS
What enterprise, Popilius?

POPILIUS   Fare you well.
           [Advances to Caesar.]

BRUTUS
What said Popilius Lena?

CASSIUS
He wished to-day our enterprise might thrive.
I fear our purpose is discoverèd.

BRUTUS
18 Look how he makes to Caesar. Mark him.

---

3 *schedule* document 7 *touches* concerns 8 *served* attended to 10
Sirrah (contemptuous form of address); *give place* get out of the way
12 s.d. *the Capitol* (possibly the 'inner stage,' probably just before it)
13 *enterprise* undertaking 18 *makes to* advances toward

72

CASSIUS
Casca, be sudden, for we fear prevention.   19
Brutus, what shall be done? If this be known,
Cassius or Caesar never shall turn back,   21
For I will slay myself.

BRUTUS   Cassius, be constant.   22
Popilius Lena speaks not of our purposes;
For look, he smiles, and Caesar doth not change.   24

CASSIUS
Trebonius knows his time; for look you, Brutus,
He draws Mark Antony out of the way.

                        [Exeunt Antony and Trebonius.]

DECIUS
Where is Metellus Cimber? Let him go
And presently prefer his suit to Caesar.   28

BRUTUS
He is addressed. Press near and second him.   29

CINNA
Casca, you are the first that rears your hand.

CAESAR
Are we all ready? What is now amiss
That Caesar and his Senate must redress?

METELLUS
Most high, most mighty, and most puissant Caesar,
Metellus Cimber throws before thy seat
An humble heart.
        [Kneels.]

CAESAR   I must prevent thee, Cimber.   35
These couchings and these lowly courtesies   36
Might fire the blood of ordinary men
And turn preordinance and first decree   38

---

19 *sudden* quick; *prevention* being forestalled   21 *turn back* return alive
22 *constant* unshaken   24 *Caesar . . . change* i.e. his expression does not
change   28 *presently* immediately; *prefer* present   29 *addressed* ready
35 *prevent* forestall   36 *couchings* bowings; *courtesies* curtsies, bowings
38 *preordinance . . . decree* the original, time-honored laws by which men
organized themselves into societies, i.e. the laws of man in accordance
with the laws of nature and of God

39 Into the lane of children. Be not fond
40 To think that Caesar bears such rebel blood
41 That will be thawed from the true quality
   With that which melteth fools – I mean, sweet words,
43 Low-crookèd curtsies, and base spaniel fawning.
   Thy brother by decree is banishèd.
   If thou dost bend and pray and fawn for him,
   I spurn thee like a cur out of my way.
47 Know, Caesar doth not wrong, nor without cause
   Will he be satisfied.

METELLUS
   Is there no voice more worthy than my own,
   To sound more sweetly in great Caesar's ear
51 For the repealing of my banished brother?

BRUTUS
   I kiss thy hand, but not in flattery, Caesar,
   Desiring thee that Publius Cimber may
54 Have an immediate freedom of repeal.

CAESAR
   What, Brutus?

CASSIUS   Pardon, Caesar! Caesar, pardon!
   As low as to thy foot doth Cassius fall
   To beg enfranchisement for Publius Cimber.

CAESAR
   I could be well moved, if I were as you;
   If I could pray to move, prayers would move me:
60 But I am constant as the Northern Star,
61 Of whose true-fixed and resting quality
62 There is no fellow in the firmament.

---

39 *lane* path, byway (many editors emend to 'law'); *fond* so foolish as
40 *rebel* untrue to its own nature   41 *thawed* i.e. altered; *true* proper
43 *spaniel* i.e. hypocritically flattering   47–48 *Know . . . satisfied* (it is possible that Shakespeare first wrote, 'Caesar did never wrong, but with just
cause, Nor without cause will he be satisfied,' but altered it out of deference
to the criticism of Ben Jonson)   51 *repealing* recalling from banishment
54 *freedom of repeal* permission to be recalled   60 *constant . . . Star* as fixed
as the polestar (an ultimate symbol of constancy)   61 *resting* immovable
62 *fellow* equal

74

The skies are painted with unnumb'red sparks,   63
They are all fire, and every one doth shine;
But there's but one in all doth hold his place.   65
So in the world : 'tis furnished well with men,
And men are flesh and blood, and apprehensive;   67
Yet in the number I do know but one
That unassailable holds on his rank,   69
Unshaked of motion; and that I am he,
Let me a little show it, even in this –
That I was constant Cimber should be banished   72
And constant do remain to keep him so.

CINNA
O Caesar.

CAESAR   Hence! Wilt thou lift up Olympus?   74

DECIUS
Great Caesar.

CAESAR   Doth not Brutus bootless kneel?   75

CASCA
Speak hands for me.
          They stab Caesar [– Casca first, Brutus last].

CAESAR
Et tu, Brutè? – Then fall Caesar.   77
          Dies.

CINNA
Liberty! Freedom! Tyranny is dead!
Run hence, proclaim, cry it about the streets!

CASSIUS
Some to the common pulpits and cry out   80
'Liberty, freedom, and enfranchisement!'

BRUTUS
People and senators, be not affrighted.
Fly not; stand still. Ambition's debt is paid.   83

63 *painted* adorned 65 *hold* remain fixed in 67 *apprehensive* capable of
knowing and reasoning 69 *holds . . . rank* remains fixed in his position 72
constant determined (resolutely) 74 *Olympus* a mountain in Greece, the
home of the gods 75 *bootless* unavailingly 77 *Et tu, Brutè* and thou, Brutus (cf. Caesar's remark at III, i, 55) 80 *pulpits* platforms for delivering
public speeches 83 *Ambition's debt* what was due to Caesar's ambition

CASCA
  Go to the pulpit, Brutus.
DECIUS   And Cassius too.
BRUTUS
85 Where's Publius?
CINNA
86 Here, quite confounded with this mutiny.
METELLUS
87 Stand fast together, lest some friend of Caesar's
    Should chance —
BRUTUS
89 Talk not of standing! Publius, good cheer.
    There is no harm intended to your person
    Nor to no Roman else. So tell them, Publius.
CASSIUS
    And leave us, Publius, lest that the people,
93 Rushing on us, should do your age some mischief.
BRUTUS
94 Do so; and let no man abide this deed
    But we the doers.
        Enter Trebonius.
CASSIUS   Where is Antony?
TREBONIUS
96 Fled to his house amazed.
    Men, wives, and children stare, cry out, and run,
    As it were doomsday.
BRUTUS   Fates, we will know your pleasures.
    That we shall die, we know; 'tis but the time,
100 And drawing days out, that men stand upon.
CASCA
    Why, he that cuts off twenty years of life
    Cuts off so many years of fearing death.

85 *Publius* an old senator, too confused to flee 86 *mutiny* tumult 87 *fast* close 89 *standing* organizing resistance 93 *your age* i.e. you as an old man 94 *abide* stand the consequences of, be responsible for 96 *amazed* full of consternation 100 *drawing ... upon* prolonging life, that men attach importance to

BRUTUS

Grant that, and then is death a benefit.
So are we Caesar's friends, that have abridged
His time of fearing death. Stoop, Romans, stoop,
And let us bathe our hands in Caesar's blood
Up to the elbows and besmear our swords.
Then walk we forth, even to the market place,   108
And waving our red weapons o'er our heads,
Let's all cry 'Peace, freedom, and liberty!'

CASSIUS

Stoop then and wash. How many ages hence
Shall this our lofty scene be acted over
In states unborn and accents yet unknown!

BRUTUS

How many times shall Caesar bleed in sport,   114
That now on Pompey's basis lies along   115
No worthier than the dust!

CASSIUS   So oft as that shall be,
So often shall the knot of us be called   117
The men that gave their country liberty.

DECIUS

What, shall we forth?   119

CASSIUS   Ay, every man away.
Brutus shall lead, and we will grace his heels   120
With the most boldest and best hearts of Rome.
            Enter a Servant.

BRUTUS

Soft! who comes here? A friend of Antony's.   122

SERVANT

Thus, Brutus, did my master bid me kneel;
Thus did Mark Antony bid me fall down;
And being prostrate, thus he bade me say:
Brutus is noble, wise, valiant, and honest;   126

---

108 *market place* the Roman Forum   114 *in sport* for entertainment, i.e.
as plays   115 *basis* pedestal of statue; *along* stretched out prostrate   117
knot group (of conspirators)   119 *forth* go out into the city   120 *grace* do
honor to   122 *Soft* wait a moment, slowly   126 *honest* honorable

127   Caesar was mighty, bold, royal, and loving.
       Say I love Brutus and I honor him;
       Say I feared Caesar, honored him, and loved him.
       If Brutus will vouchsafe that Antony
131   May safely come to him and be resolved
       How Caesar hath deserved to lie in death,
       Mark Antony shall not love Caesar dead
       So well as Brutus living; but will follow
       The fortunes and affairs of noble Brutus
136   Thorough the hazards of this untrod state
       With all true faith. So says my master Antony.

BRUTUS
       Thy master is a wise and valiant Roman.
       I never thought him worse.
140   Tell him, so please him come unto this place,
       He shall be satisfied and, by my honor,
       Depart untouched.

SERVANT   I'll fetch him presently.   *Exit.*

BRUTUS
143   I know that we shall have him well to friend.

CASSIUS
144   I wish we may. But yet have I a mind
145   That fears him much; and my misgiving still
146   Falls shrewdly to the purpose.
                 Enter Antony.

BRUTUS
       But here comes Antony. Welcome, Mark Antony.

ANTONY
       O mighty Caesar! dost thou lie so low?
       Are all thy conquests, glories, triumphs, spoils,
       Shrunk to this little measure? Fare thee well.
       I know not, gentlemen, what you intend,

127 *royal* nobly munificent   131 *be resolved* have satisfactorily explained to him (?), be fully informed (?)   136 *Thorough* (common dissyllabic form of 'through'); *untrod state* novel state of affairs (?), uncertain future (?)   140 *so* if it should   143 *to* as a   144 *mind* presentiment   145 *fears* distrusts; *still* always   146 *Falls . . . purpose* turns out to be very near the truth

Who else must be let blood, who else is rank.   152
If I myself, there is no hour so fit
As Caesar's death's hour; nor no instrument
Of half that worth as those your swords, made rich
With the most noble blood of all this world.
I do beseech ye, if you bear me hard,   157
Now, whilst your purpled hands do reek and smoke,   158
Fulfil your pleasure. Live a thousand years,   159
I shall not find myself so apt to die;   160
No place will please me so, no mean of death,   161
As here by Caesar, and by you cut off,
The choice and master spirits of this age.

BRUTUS
O Antony, beg not your death of us!
Though now we must appear bloody and cruel,
As by our hands and this our present act
You see we do, yet see you but our hands
And this the bleeding business they have done.
Our hearts you see not. They are pitiful;   169
And pity to the general wrong of Rome
(As fire drives out fire, so pity pity)   171
Hath done this deed on Caesar. For your part,
To you our swords have leaden points, Mark Antony.
Our arms in strength of malice, and our hearts   174
Of brothers' temper, do receive you in
With all kind love, good thoughts, and reverence.

CASSIUS
Your voice shall be as strong as any man's   177
In the disposing of new dignities.   178

BRUTUS

Only be patient till we have appeased
The multitude, beside themselves with fear,
181   And then we will deliver you the cause
Why I, that did love Caesar when I struck him,
Have thus proceeded.

ANTONY   I doubt not of your wisdom.
Let each man render me his bloody hand.
First, Marcus Brutus, will I shake with you ;
Next, Caius Cassius, do I take your hand ;
Now, Decius Brutus, yours ; now yours, Metellus ;
Yours, Cinna ; and, my valiant Casca, yours.
Though last, not least in love, yours, good Trebonius.
Gentlemen all – Alas, what shall I say ?
191   My credit now stands on such slippery ground
192   That one of two bad ways you must conceit me,
Either a coward or a flatterer.
That I did love thee, Caesar, O, ’tis true !
If then thy spirit look upon us now,
196   Shall it not grieve thee dearer than thy death
To see thy Antony making his peace,
Shaking the bloody fingers of thy foes,
Most noble ! in the presence of thy corse ?
Had I as many eyes as thou hast wounds,
Weeping as fast as they stream forth thy blood,
202   It would become me better than to close
In terms of friendship with thine enemies.
204   Pardon me, Julius ! Here wast thou bayed, brave hart ;
Here didst thou fall ; and here thy hunters stand,
206   Signed in thy spoil, and crimsoned in thy lethe.
O world, thou wast the forest to this hart ;
And this indeed, O world, the heart of thee !

---

181 *deliver* report to   191 *My credit* my reputation as Caesar's friend (?),
trust in me (?)   192 *conceit* judge   196 *dearer* more keenly   202 *close*
conclude an agreement   204 *bayed* brought to bay ; *hart* deer (with pun on
'heart')   206 *Signed . . . spoil* marked with the signs of your slaughter;
lethe deer's blood, marked on all who were in at the kill (disyllabic)

How like a deer, stroken by many princes,   209
Dost thou here lie!

CASSIUS
Mark Antony —

ANTONY   Pardon me, Caius Cassius.
The enemies of Caesar shall say this;
Then, in a friend, it is cold modesty.   213

CASSIUS
I blame you not for praising Caesar so;   *WILL YOU JOIN US*
But what compact mean you to have with us?   215
Will you be pricked in number of our friends,   216
Or shall we on, and not depend on you?

ANTONY
Therefore I took your hands, but was indeed
Swayed from the point by looking down on Caesar.
Friends am I with you all, and love you all,   *ONLY IF REASONS*
Upon this hope, that you shall give me reasons   *NOT A FIRM*
Why and wherein Caesar was dangerous.   *COMMITMENT*

BRUTUS
Or else were this a savage spectacle.
Our reasons are so full of good regard   224
That were you, Antony, the son of Caesar,
You should be satisfied.

ANTONY   That's all I seek;
And am moreover suitor that I may
Produce his body to the market place   228
And in the pulpit, as becomes a friend,
Speak in the order of his funeral.   230

BRUTUS
You shall, Mark Antony.

CASSIUS   Brutus, a word with you.
        [Aside to Brutus]
You know not what you do. Do not consent

---

209 *stroken* struck down 213 *modesty* moderation 215 *compact* agreement
(accented on second syllable) 216 *pricked* marked down 224 *good regard*
sound considerations 228 *Produce* bring forth 230 *order* ritual, ceremony

That Antony speak in his funeral.
Know you how much the people may be moved
By that which he will utter ?

BRUTUS *[aside to Cassius]*   By your pardon –
I will myself into the pulpit first
And show the reason of our Caesar's death.

238   What Antony shall speak, I will protest
He speaks by leave and by permission ;
And that we are contented Caesar shall

241   Have all true rites and lawful ceremonies.   *LOOK*
242   It shall advantage more than do us wrong.   *GOOD TO PUBLIC*

CASSIUS *[aside to Brutus]*

243   I know not what may fall. I like it not.

BRUTUS
Mark Antony, here, take you Caesar's body.
You shall not in your funeral speech blame us,
But speak all good you can devise of Caesar ;
And say you do't by our permission.
Else shall you not have any hand at all
About his funeral. And you shall speak
In the same pulpit whereto I am going,
After my speech is ended.

ANTONY   Be it so.
I do desire no more.

BRUTUS
Prepare the body then, and follow us.

                              Exeunt. Manet Antony.

ANTONY
ALONE   O, pardon me, thou bleeding piece of earth,
That I am meek and gentle with these butchers !
Thou art the ruins of the noblest man
257   That ever livèd in the tide of times.
Woe to the hand that shed this costly blood !
Over thy wounds now do I prophesy
(Which, like dumb mouths, do ope their ruby lips

238 *protest* proclaim   241 *true* proper   242 *advantage* benefit (us)   243
fall happen   257 *tide of times* course of history

82

To beg the voice and utterance of my tongue),
A curse shall light upon the limbs of men ;
Domestic fury and fierce civil strife
Shall cumber all the parts of Italy ;   264
Blood and destruction shall be so in use   265
And dreadful objects so familiar
That mothers shall but smile when they behold
Their infants quarterèd with the hands of war,
All pity choked with custom of fell deeds ;   269
And Caesar's spirit, ranging for revenge,   270
With Atè by his side come hot from hell,   271
Shall in these confines with a monarch's voice   272
Cry 'Havoc!' and let slip the dogs of war,   273
That this foul deed shall smell above the earth   274
With carrion men, groaning for burial.   275
  Enter Octavius' Servant.
You serve Octavius Caesar, do you not ?

SERVANT
I do, Mark Antony.

ANTONY
Caesar did write for him to come to Rome.

SERVANT
He did receive his letters and is coming,
And bid me say to you by word of mouth –
O Caesar !

ANTONY
Thy heart is big. Get thee apart and weep.   282
Passion, I see, is catching ; for mine eyes,   283
Seeing those beads of sorrow stand in thine,
Began to water. Is thy master coming ?

SERVANT
He lies to-night within seven leagues of Rome.

---

264 *cumber* burden   265 *in use* common   269 *custom . . . deeds* being
accustomed to cruel deeds   270 *ranging* roving (in search of prey)   271
Atè Greek goddess of discord   272 *confines* regions   273 *Havoc* the signal
for unlimited slaughter; *let slip* unleash   274 *That* so that   275 *carrion*
dead and rotting   282 *big* full of grief   283 *Passion* grief

ANTONY

287   Post back with speed and tell him what hath chanced.
       Here is a mourning Rome, a dangerous Rome,
289   No Rome of safety for Octavius yet.
290   Hie hence and tell him so. Yet stay awhile.
       Thou shalt not back till I have borne this corse
292   Into the market place. There shall I try
       In my oration how the people take
294   The cruel issue of these bloody men;
295   According to the which thou shalt discourse
       To young Octavius of the state of things.
       Lend me your hand.   *Exeunt [with Caesar's body].*

5 DAYS PASS— CONSPIRATORS
DIVIDE UP EMPIRE

III, ii   *Enter Brutus and [presently] goes into the pulpit,
                   and Cassius, with the Plebeians.*

PLEBEIANS

1   We will be satisfied! Let us be satisfied!

BRUTUS

2   Then follow me and give me audience, friends.
       Cassius, go you into the other street
4   And part the numbers.
       Those that will hear me speak, let 'em stay here;
       Those that will follow Cassius, go with him;
7   And public reasons shall be renderèd
       Of Caesar's death.

1. PLEBEIAN   I will hear Brutus speak.

2. PLEBEIAN
       I will hear Cassius, and compare their reasons
10   When severally we hear them renderèd.
                   [Exit Cassius, with some of the Plebeians.]

287 *chanced* happened   289 *Rome* (see I, ii, 156n.)   290 *Hie* hasten   292
try test   294 *cruel issue* result of the cruelty   295 *the which* the result of my
test

III, ii The Forum   1 *will be satisfied* demand a full explanation   2 *audience*
a hearing   4 *part* divide   7 *public reasons* reasons having to do with the
general good (?), reasons in explanation to the public (?)   10 *severally*
separately

84

3. PLEBEIAN
The noble Brutus is ascended. Silence!

BRUTUS Be patient till the last.   12

Romans, countrymen, and lovers, hear me for my cause,   13
and be silent, that you may hear. Believe me for mine
honor, and have respect to mine honor, that you may   15
believe. Censure me in your wisdom, and awake your   16
senses, that you may the better judge. If there be any in   17
this assembly, any dear friend of Caesar's, to him I say
that Brutus' love to Caesar was no less than his. If then
that friend demand why Brutus rose against Caesar, this
is my answer: Not that I loved Caesar less, but that I
loved Rome more. Had you rather Caesar were living,
and die all slaves, than that Caesar were dead, to live all
freemen? As Caesar loved me, I weep for him; as he was
fortunate, I rejoice at it; as he was valiant, I honor him;
but – as he was ambitious, I slew him. There is tears for
his love; joy for his fortune; honor for his valor; and
death for his ambition. Who is here so base that would
be a bondman? If any, speak; for him have I offended.   29
Who is here so rude that would not be a Roman? If any,   30
speak; for him have I offended. Who is here so vile that
will not love his country? If any, speak; for him have I
offended. I pause for a reply.

ALL None, Brutus, none!

BRUTUS Then none have I offended. I have done no more
to Caesar than you shall do to Brutus. The question of   36
his death is enrolled in the Capitol; his glory not extenu-   37
ated, wherein he was worthy; nor his offenses enforced,   38
for which he suffered death.

> *Enter Mark Antony [and others], with Caesar's
> body.*

12 *last* end of my speech   13 *lovers* dear friends; *my cause* i.e. the cause of
freedom   15 *have . . . honor* remember that I am honorable   16 *Censure*
judge   17 *senses* reason   29 *bondman* slave   30 *rude* barbarous   36 *shall
do* i.e. if Brutus should so offend; *question of* considerations that led to   37
enrolled in recorded in the archives of; *extenuated* understated   38 *enforced*
overstated

Here comes his body, mourned by Mark Antony, who,
though he had no hand in his death, shall receive the
42 benefit of his dying, a place in the commonwealth, as
which of you shall not ? With this I depart, that, as I slew
44 my best lover for the good of Rome, I have the same
dagger for myself when it shall please my country to
need my death.

ALL Live, Brutus ! live, live !

1 . PLEBEIAN
Bring him with triumph home unto his house.

2 . PLEBEIAN
49 Give him a statue with his ancestors.

3 . PLEBEIAN
Let him be Caesar. ~~BRUTUS DICTATOR?~~

4 . PLEBEIAN   Caesar's better parts
Shall be crowned in Brutus.

1 . PLEBEIAN
We'll bring him to his house with shouts and clamors.

BRUTUS
My countrymen –

2 . PLEBEIAN   Peace ! silence ! Brutus speaks.

1 . PLEBEIAN Peace, ho !

BRUTUS
Good countrymen, let me depart alone,
And, for my sake, stay here with Antony.
57 Do grace to Caesar's corpse, and grace his speech
58 Tending to Caesar's glories which Mark Antony,
By our permission, is allowed to make.
I do entreat you, not a man depart,
Save I alone, till Antony have spoke.   *Exit*.

1 . PLEBEIAN
Stay, ho ! and let us hear Mark Antony.

3 . PLEBEIAN
63 Let him go up into the public chair.

42 *place* i.e. as a free Roman   44 *lover* friend   49 *ancestors* (see I, ii, 159n.)
57 *Do . . . speech* show due respect to Caesar's corpse and listen respectfully
to Antony's speech   58 *Tending* relating   63 *chair* pulpit, rostrum

We'll hear him. Noble Antony, go up.

ANTONY

For Brutus' sake I am beholding to you. 65

[Antony goes into the pulpit.]

4 . PLEBEIAN

What does he say of Brutus?

3 . PLEBEIAN He says for Brutus' sake
He finds himself beholding to us all.

4 . PLEBEIAN

'Twere best he speak no harm of Brutus here!

1 . PLEBEIAN

This Caesar was a tyrant.

3 . PLEBEIAN Nay, that's certain.
We are blest that Rome is rid of him.

2 . PLEBEIAN

Peace! Let us hear what Antony can say.

ANTONY

You gentle Romans –

ALL Peace, ho! Let us hear him.

ANTONY

Friends, Romans, countrymen, lend me your ears;
I come to bury Caesar, not to praise him.
The evil that men do lives after them;
The good is oft interrèd with their bones.
So let it be with Caesar. The noble Brutus
Hath told you Caesar was ambitious.
If it were so, it was a grievous fault,
And grievously hath Caesar answered it. 80
Here under leave of Brutus and the rest
(For Brutus is an honorable man;
So are they all, all honorable men),
Come I to speak in Caesar's funeral.
He was my friend, faithful and just to me; 85
But Brutus says he was ambitious,
And Brutus is an honorable man.

65 *beholding* obliged 80 *answered it* paid the penalty 85 *just* entirely
reliable

He hath brought many captives home to Rome,
89   Whose ransoms did the general coffers fill.
Did this in Caesar seem ambitious?
When that the poor have cried, Caesar hath wept;
Ambition should be made of sterner stuff.
Yet Brutus says he was ambitious;
And Brutus is an honorable man.
You all did see that on the Lupercal
I thrice presented him a kingly crown,
Which he did thrice refuse. Was this ambition?
Yet Brutus says he was ambitious;
And sure he is an honorable man.
100   I speak not to disprove what Brutus spoke,
But here I am to speak what I do know.
You all did love him once, not without cause.
What cause withholds you then to mourn for him?
O judgment, thou art fled to brutish beasts,
And men have lost their reason! Bear with me.
My heart is in the coffin there with Caesar,
And I must pause till it come back to me.

1. PLEBEIAN
Methinks there is much reason in his sayings.

2. PLEBEIAN
If thou consider rightly of the matter,
Caesar has had great wrong.

3. PLEBEIAN   Has he, masters?
I fear there will a worse come in his place.

4. PLEBEIAN
Marked ye his words? He would not take the crown;
Therefore 'tis certain he was not ambitious.

1. PLEBEIAN
114   If it be found so, some will dear abide it.

2. PLEBEIAN
Poor soul! his eyes are red as fire with weeping.

89 *general coffers* public treasury   114 *dear abide it* pay a heavy penalty for it

3. PLEBEIAN
There's not a nobler man in Rome than Antony.

4. PLEBEIAN
Now mark him. He begins again to speak.

ANTONY
But yesterday the word of Caesar might
Have stood against the world. Now lies he there,
And none so poor to do him reverence.   120
O masters! If I were disposed to stir
Your hearts and minds to mutiny and rage,   122
I should do Brutus wrong, and Cassius wrong,
Who, you all know, are honorable men.
I will not do them wrong. I rather choose
To wrong the dead, to wrong myself and you,
Than I will wrong such honorable men.
But here's a parchment with the seal of Caesar.
I found it in his closet; 'tis his will.   129
Let but the commons hear this testament,   130
Which (pardon me) I do not mean to read,
And they would go and kiss dead Caesar's wounds
And dip their napkins in his sacred blood;   133
Yea, beg a hair of him for memory,
And dying, mention it within their wills,
Bequeathing it as a rich legacy
Unto their issue.

4. PLEBEIAN
We'll hear the will! Read it, Mark Antony.

ALL
The will, the will! We will hear Caesar's will!

ANTONY
Have patience, gentle friends; I must not read it.
It is not meet you know how Caesar loved you.   141
You are not wood, you are not stones, but men;

---

120 *so poor* base enough   122 *mutiny* riot   129 *closet* study (?), cabinet for
private papers (?)   130 *commons* plebeians   133 *napkins* handkerchiefs
141 *meet* fitting that

And being men, hearing the will of Caesar,
It will inflame you, it will make you mad.
'Tis good you know not that you are his heirs;
For if you should, O, what would come of it?

4 . PLEBEIAN
Read the will! We'll hear it, Antony!
You shall read us the will, Caesar's will!

ANTONY
149 Will you be patient? Will you stay awhile?
150 I have o'ershot myself to tell you of it.
I fear I wrong the honorable men
Whose daggers have stabbed Caesar; I do fear it.

4 . PLEBEIAN
They were traitors. Honorable men!

ALL
The will! the testament!

2 . PLEBEIAN   They were villains,
Murderers! The will! Read the will!

ANTONY
You will compel me then to read the will?
Then make a ring about the corpse of Caesar
And let me show you him that made the will.
Shall I descend? and will you give me leave?

ALL Come down.

2 . PLEBEIAN Descend.

3 . PLEBEIAN You shall have leave.
   [Antony comes down.]

4 . PLEBEIAN A ring! Stand round.

1 . PLEBEIAN
165 Stand from the hearse! Stand from the body!

2 . PLEBEIAN
Room for Antony, most noble Antony!

ANTONY
167 Nay, press not so upon me. Stand far off.

168 ALL Stand back! Room! Bear back!

---

149 *stay* wait 150 *o'ershot myself* gone further than I intended 165
hearse bier 167 *far* farther 168 *Bear* move

ANTONY
    If you have tears, prepare to shed them now.
    You all do know this mantle. I remember   170
    The first time ever Caesar put it on.
    'Twas on a summer's evening in his tent,
    That day he overcame the Nervii.   173
    Look, in this place ran Cassius' dagger through.
    See what a rent the envious Casca made.   175
    Through this the well-belovèd Brutus stabbed;
    And as he plucked his cursèd steel away,
    Mark how the blood of Caesar followed it,
    As rushing out of doors to be resolved   179
    If Brutus so unkindly knocked or no;   180
    For Brutus, as you know, was Caesar's angel.   181
    Judge, O you gods, how dearly Caesar loved him!
    This was the most unkindest cut of all;   183
    For when the noble Caesar saw him stab,
    Ingratitude, more strong than traitors' arms,
    Quite vanquished him. Then burst his mighty heart;
    And in his mantle muffling up his face,
    Even at the base of Pompey's statue   188
    (Which all the while ran blood) great Caesar fell.
    O, what a fall was there, my countrymen!
    Then I, and you, and all of us fell down,
    Whilst bloody treason flourished over us.   192
    O, now you weep, and I perceive you feel
    The dint of pity. These are gracious drops.   194
    Kind souls, what weep you when you but behold   195
    Our Caesar's vesture wounded? Look you here!   196
    Here is himself, marred as you see with traitors.   197

170 *mantle* cloak (here toga)   173 *Nervii* a tribe defeated in 57 B.C. in one
of the most decisive victories in the Gallic Wars   175 *envious* malicious
179 *be resolved* learn for certain   180 *unkindly* unnaturally and cruelly   181
angel 'darling,' i.e. favorite who could do no wrong   183 *most unkindest*
cruelest and most unnatural   188 *base* pedestal; *statue* (trisyllabic)   192
flourished swaggered and brandished its sword in triumph   194 *dint*
impression; *gracious* full of grace, becoming   195 *what* why   196 *vesture*
i.e. the mantle   197 *marred* mangled; *with* by

 1 . PLEBEIAN O piteous spectacle!

 2 . PLEBEIAN O noble Caesar!

 3 . PLEBEIAN O woeful day!

 4 . PLEBEIAN O traitors, villains!

 1 . PLEBEIAN O most bloody sight!

 2 . PLEBEIAN We will be revenged.

204 [ALL] Revenge! About! Seek! Burn! Fire! Kill! Slay!
     Let not a traitor live!

206 ANTONY Stay, countrymen.

 1 . PLEBEIAN Peace there! Hear the noble Antony.

 2 . PLEBEIAN We'll hear him, we'll follow him, we'll die
     with him!

ANTONY

    Good friends, sweet friends, let me not stir you up
    To such a sudden flood of mutiny.
    They that have done this deed are honorable.

213 What private griefs they have, alas, I know not,
    That made them do it. They are wise and honorable,
    And will no doubt with reasons answer you.
    I come not, friends, to steal away your hearts.
    I am no orator, as Brutus is,
    But (as you know me all) a plain blunt man
    That love my friend; and that they know full well

220 That gave me public leave to speak of him.

221 For I have neither writ, nor words, nor worth,

222 Action, nor utterance, nor the power of speech

223 To stir men's blood. I only speak right on.
    I tell you that which you yourselves do know,
    Show you sweet Caesar's wounds, poor poor dumb
        mouths,
    And bid them speak for me. But were I Brutus,

---

204 *About* to work 206 *Stay* wait 213 *private griefs* personal grievances
220 *public . . . speak* permission to speak in public 221 *writ* a written-out
speech (most editors emend to 'wit,' i.e. invention, which accords with
the rest of the list of qualities of a good orator that follows); *words* fluency;
worth stature as a public figure, authority 222 *Action* skilful use of
gesture; *utterance* good delivery 223 *right on* straight out, just as I think it

And Brutus Antony, there were an Antony
Would ruffle up your spirits, and put a tongue   228
In every wound of Caesar that should move
The stones of Rome to rise and mutiny.

ALL
  We'll mutiny.

1. PLEBEIAN   We'll burn the house of Brutus.

3. PLEBEIAN
  Away then! Come, seek the conspirators.

ANTONY
  Yet hear me, countrymen. Yet hear me speak.

ALL
  Peace, ho! Hear Antony, most noble Antony!

ANTONY
  Why, friends, you go to do you know not what.
  Wherein hath Caesar thus deserved your loves?
  Alas, you know not! I must tell you then.
  You have forgot the will I told you of.

ALL
  Most true! The will! Let's stay and hear the will.

ANTONY
  Here is the will, and under Caesar's seal.
  To every Roman citizen he gives,
  To every several man, seventy-five drachmas.   242

2. PLEBEIAN
  Most noble Caesar! We'll revenge his death!

3. PLEBEIAN   O royal Caesar!   244

ANTONY   Hear me with patience.

ALL   Peace, ho!

ANTONY
  Moreover, he hath left you all his walks,   247
  His private arbors, and new-planted orchards,   248
  On this side Tiber; he hath left them you,
  And to your heirs for ever – common pleasures,   250

228 *ruffle up* stir to rage   242 *several* individual; *seventy-five drachmas* (at least £12 to-day)   244 *royal* nobly munificent   247 *walks* (see I, ii, 155n.) 248 *orchards* gardens   250 *common pleasures* public parks

To walk abroad and recreate yourselves.
Here was a Caesar! When comes such another?

1 . PLEBEIAN
Never, never! Come, away, away!
254   We'll burn his body in the holy place
And with the brands fire the traitors' houses.
Take up the body.

2 . PLEBEIAN   Go fetch fire!

258   3 . PLEBEIAN   Pluck down benches!

259   4 . PLEBEIAN   Pluck down forms, windows, anything!

Exit Plebeians [with the body].

ANTONY
260   Now let it work. Mischief, thou art afoot,
Take thou what course thou wilt.
261   *Enter Servant.*   How now, fellow?

SERVANT
Sir, Octavius is already come to Rome.

ANTONY   Where is he?

SERVANT
He and Lepidus are at Caesar's house.

ANTONY
265   And thither will I straight to visit him.
266   He comes upon a wish. Fortune is merry,
And in this mood will give us anything.

SERVANT
I heard him say Brutus and Cassius
269   Are rid like madmen through the gates of Rome.

ANTONY
270   Belike they had some notice of the people,
271   How I had moved them. Bring me to Octavius.   *Exeunt.*

*

254 *holy place* where the most sacred temples were in Rome   258 *Pluck down* wrench loose, tear out   259 *forms* long benches; *windows* shutters
260 *work* have its full effect   261 *fellow* (form of address to inferiors)
265 *straight* at once   266 *upon a wish* exactly as I might have wished; *merry* in a good mood (toward us)   269 *Are rid* have ridden   270 *Belike* probably; *notice of* news about   271 *Bring* escort

Enter Cinna the Poet, and after him the Plebeians. III, iii

CINNA

I dreamt to-night that I did feast with Caesar, 1
And things unluckily charge my fantasy. 2
I have no will to wander forth of doors, 3
Yet something leads me forth.

1. PLEBEIAN What is your name?

2. PLEBEIAN Whither are you going?

3. PLEBEIAN Where do you dwell?

4. PLEBEIAN Are you a married man or a bachelor?

2. PLEBEIAN Answer every man directly. 9

1. PLEBEIAN Ay, and briefly.

4. PLEBEIAN Ay, and wisely.

3. PLEBEIAN Ay, and truly, you were best.

CINNA What is my name? Whither am I going? Where
do I dwell? Am I a married man or a bachelor? Then,
to answer every man directly and briefly, wisely and
truly: wisely I say, I am a bachelor.

2. PLEBEIAN That's as much as to say they are fools that 17
marry. You'll bear me a bang for that, I fear. Proceed 18
directly.

CINNA Directly I am going to Caesar's funeral.

1. PLEBEIAN As a friend or an enemy?

CINNA As a friend.

2. PLEBEIAN That matter is answered directly.

4. PLEBEIAN For your dwelling – briefly.

CINNA Briefly, I dwell by the Capitol.

3. PLEBEIAN Your name, sir, truly.

CINNA Truly, my name is Cinna.

1. PLEBEIAN Tear him to pieces! He's a conspirator.

CINNA I am Cinna the poet! I am Cinna the poet!

4. PLEBEIAN Tear him for his bad verses! Tear him for
his bad verses!

CINNA I am not Cinna the conspirator.

III, iii A street 1 *to-night* last night 2 *things . . . fantasy* what has happened
gives my dream a bad interpretation 3 *forth* out 9 *directly* plainly
17–18 *they . . . marry* (proverbial) 18 *bear me a bang* get a beating from me

33 4. PLEBEIAN It is no matter; his name 's Cinna! Pluck
34   but his name out of his heart, and turn him going.

    3. PLEBEIAN Tear him, tear him! *[They kill him.]* Come,
       brands, ho! firebrands! To Brutus', to Cassius'! Burn
       all! Some to Decius' house and some to Casca's; some
       to Ligarius'! Away, go!

                    Exeunt all the Plebeians [with the body of Cinna].

1½ yrs. HAVE ELAPSED
CICERO HATED ANTONY

IV, i   *Enter Antony, Octavius, and Lepidus.*

    ANTONY
1   These many, then, shall die; their names are pricked.
    OCTAVIUS
       Your brother too must die. Consent you, Lepidus?
    LEPIDUS
       I do consent –
    OCTAVIUS   Prick him down, Antony.
    LEPIDUS
       Upon condition Publius shall not live,
       Who is your sister's son, Mark Antony.

ANTONY'S NEPHEW

    ANTONY
6   He shall not live. Look, with a spot I damn him.
       But, Lepidus, go you to Caesar's house.
       Fetch the will hither, and we shall determine
9   How to cut off some charge in legacies.

USING PEOPLES MONEY FOR OWN PURPOSES

    LEPIDUS
       What? shall I find you here?
    OCTAVIUS
11 Or here or at the Capitol.   *Exit Lepidus.*
    ANTONY
12 This is a slight unmeritable man,
       Meet to be sent on errands. Is it fit,

---

33 *Pluck* tear   34 *turn him going* send him packing
IV, i The house of Antony   1 *pricked* marked down on a list   6 *spot* mark;
damn condemn   9 *cut . . . charge* reduce the outlay of the estate (by altering
the will)   11 *Or* either   12 *slight unmeritable* insignificant and unworthy

The threefold world divided, he should stand   14
One of the three to share it?

OCTAVIUS   So you thought him,
And took his voice who should be pricked to die   16
In our black sentence and proscription.   17

ANTONY
Octavius, I have seen more days than you;   18
And though we lay these honors on this man
To ease ourselves of divers sland'rous loads,
He shall but bear them as the ass bears gold,   20
To groan and sweat under the business,   22
Either led or driven as we point the way;
And having brought our treasure where we will,
Then take we down his load, and turn him off   25
(Like to the empty ass) to shake his ears   26
And graze in commons.   27

OCTAVIUS   You may do your will;
But he's a tried and valiant soldier.   28

ANTONY
So is my horse, Octavius, and for that
I do appoint him store of provender.   30
It is a creature that I teach to fight,
To wind, to stop, to run directly on,   32
His corporal motion governed by my spirit.   33
And, in some taste, is Lepidus but so.   34
He must be taught, and trained, and bid go forth:
A barren-spirited fellow; one that feeds   36
On objects, arts, and imitations

---

14 *The . . . divided* world being divided among the three triumvirs into
three parts (Europe, Africa, and Asia)   16 *voice* vote   17 *black* i.e. death;
proscription condemnation to death or exile   18 *have . . . days* am older,
i.e. more experienced   20 *ease . . . loads* lighten for ourselves some of the
charges that will be brought against us   22 *business* work done by beasts
25 *turn him off* send him packing   26 *empty* unburdened   27 *commons*
public pasture   28 *soldier* (trisyllabic)   30 *appoint* assign; *store* a supply
32 *To wind . . . on* to turn, to stop suddenly, to resume running immediately
33 *corporal* bodily   34 *taste* degree; *so* the same   36 *barren-spirited*
without initiative, unoriginal   36–37 *feeds . . . imitations* nourishes his
spirit with curiosities, artificial contrivances, and following of fashions

38   Which, out of use and staled by other men,
39   Begin his fashion. Do not talk of him
40   But as a property. And now, Octavius,
41   Listen great things. Brutus and Cassius
42   Are levying powers. We must straight make head.
43   Therefore let our alliance be combined,
44   Our best friends made, our means stretched;
      And let us presently go sit in council
46   How covert matters may be best disclosed
47   And open perils surest answerèd.
      OCTAVIUS
48   Let us do so; for we are at the stake
      And bayed about with many enemies;
      And some that smile have in their hearts, I fear,
51   Millions of mischiefs.   *Exeunt.*

IV, ii   *Drum. Enter Brutus, Lucilius, [Lucius,] and the*
                Army. Titinius and Pindarus meet them.
      BRUTUS Stand ho!
      LUCILIUS Give the word, ho! and stand!
      BRUTUS
          What now, Lucilius! Is Cassius near?
      LUCILIUS
          He is at hand, and Pindarus is come
          To do you salutation from his master.
      BRUTUS
6   He greets me well. Your master, Pindarus,

38 *staled* cheapened, worn-out   39 *Begin his fashion* he then adopts as
fashionable   40 *property* chattel (?), tool (?)   41 *Listen* hear   42 *straight
make head* immediately raise an army   43 *combined* strengthened   44
made mustered; *stretched* used to their fullest advantage   46 *How . . .
disclosed* to determine how hidden dangers may best be discovered   47
surest answerèd most safely met   48 *at the stake* i.e. like a bear at the stake
bayed by dogs   51 *mischiefs* schemes to harm us
IV, ii The camp of Brutus (near Sardis)   6 *greets me well* sends his greetings
by a worthy man

In his own change, or by ill officers,   7
Hath given me some worthy cause to wish   8
Things done undone; but if he be at hand,
I shall be satisfied.   10

PINDARUS   I do not doubt
But that my noble master will appear
Such as he is, full of regard and honor.   12

BRUTUS

He is not doubted. A word, Lucilius,   13
How he received you. Let me be resolved.   14

LUCILIUS

With courtesy and with respect enough,
But not with such familiar instances   16
Nor with such free and friendly conference   17
As he hath used of old.

BRUTUS   Thou hast described
A hot friend cooling. Ever note, Lucilius,   19
When love begins to sicken and decay
It useth an enforcèd ceremony.   21
There are no tricks in plain and simple faith;
But hollow men, like horses hot at hand,   23
Make gallant show and promise of their mettle;   24
          Low march within.
But when they should endure the bloody spur,
They fall their crests, and like deceitful jades   26
Sink in the trial. Comes his army on?   27

LUCILIUS

They mean this night in Sardis to be quartered.   28

---

7 *In . . . officers* whether from changed feelings on his part or through the
acts of unworthy subordinates 8 *worthy* justifiable 10 *be satisfied*
receive a full explanation 12 *Such* exactly; *full . . . honor* regardful (of
your interests) and honorable 13 *A word* i.e. tell me 14 *resolved* fully
informed 16 *familiar instances* signs of friendship 17 *conference* con-
versation 19 *Ever note* always observe 21 *enforcèd* forced 23 *hollow*
insincere; *hot at hand* spirited at the start 24 *mettle* high spirit 26 *fall* let
fall; *crests* ridges of horses' necks; *jades* horses (contemptuous) 27 *Sink
. . . trial* fail when they are put to the test 28 *Sardis* (the capital of the
ancient kingdom of Lydia, in western Asia Minor; Brutus had requested
Cassius to join forces with him there)

29   The greater part, the horse in general,
        Are come with Cassius.
BRUTUS   Hark! He is arrived.
31   March gently on to meet him.
                    Enter Cassius and his Powers.
CASSIUS Stand, ho!
BRUTUS Stand, ho! Speak the word along.
1. SOLDIER Stand!
2. SOLDIER Stand!
3. SOLDIER Stand!
CASSIUS
        Most noble brother, you have done me wrong.
BRUTUS
        Judge me, you gods! wrong I mine enemies?
        And if not so, how should I wrong a brother.
CASSIUS
40   Brutus, this sober form of yours hides wrongs;
        And when you do them –
41 **BRUTUS**   Cassius, be content.
42   Speak your griefs softly. I do know you well.
        Before the eyes of both our armies here
        (Which should perceive nothing but love from us)
        Let us not wrangle. Bid them move away.
46   Then in my tent, Cassius, enlarge your griefs,
47   And I will give you audience.
CASSIUS   Pindarus,
48   Bid our commanders lead their charges off
        A little from this ground.
BRUTUS
        Lucilius, do you the like; and let no man
        Come to our tent till we have done our conference.
        Let Lucius and Titinius guard our door.
                                        Exeunt.

---

29 *horse in general* all the cavalry   31 *gently* slowly   40 *sober form* serious
and restrained manner   41 *content* calm   42 *griefs* grievances   46 *enlarge*
expound fully   47 *audience* a hearing   48 *charges* troops

Mane[n]t Brutus and Cassius.   IV, iii

CASSIUS

That you have wronged me doth appear in this:
You have condemned and noted Lucius Pella   2
For taking bribes here of the Sardians;
Wherein my letters, praying on his side,   4
Because I knew the man, was slighted off.   5

BRUTUS

You wronged yourself to write in such a case.

CASSIUS

In such a time as this it is not meet
That every nice offense should bear his comment.   8

BRUTUS

Let me tell you, Cassius, you yourself
Are much condemned to have an itching palm,   10
To sell and mart your offices for gold   11
To undeservers.

CASSIUS   I an itching palm?
You know that you are Brutus that speaks this,
Or, by the gods, this speech were else your last!

BRUTUS

The name of Cassius honors this corruption,   15
And chastisement doth therefore hide his head.

CASSIUS Chastisement?

BRUTUS

Remember March; the ides of March remember.
Did not great Julius bleed for justice sake?
What villain touched his body that did stab
And not for justice? What, shall one of us,   21
That struck the foremost man of all this world
But for supporting robbers – shall we now   23

IV, iii **2** *noted* publicly disgraced, slandered **4** *letters* (singular in meaning) **5** *slighted off* contemptuously dismissed **8** *nice . . . comment* trivial
offense should be criticized **10** *condemned to have* accused of having; *itching
palm* i.e. a covetous disposition **11** *mart* traffic in **15** *honors* lends an appearance of honor to **21** *And not* except **23** *supporting robbers* i.e. having
backed those who desire to rob the Romans of their freedom (see I, ii, 283n.)

Contaminate our fingers with base bribes,
25 And sell the mighty space of our large honors
26 For so much trash as may be graspèd thus?
27 I had rather be a dog and bay the moon
    Than such a Roman.
28 CASSIUS   Brutus, bait not me!
    I'll not endure it. You forget yourself
30 To hedge me in. I am a soldier, I,
    Older in practice, abler than yourself
32 To make conditions.
    BRUTUS   Go to! You are not Cassius.
    CASSIUS I am.
    BRUTUS I say you are not.
    CASSIUS
35 Urge me no more! I shall forget myself.
36 Have mind upon your health. Tempt me no farther.
37 BRUTUS Away, slight man!
    CASSIUS
    Is't possible?
    BRUTUS   Hear me, for I will speak.
39 Must I give way and room to your rash choler?
40 Shall I be frighted when a madman stares?
    CASSIUS
    O ye gods, ye gods! Must I endure all this?
    BRUTUS
    All this? Ay, more! Fret till your proud heart break.
    Go show your slaves how choleric you are
44 And make your bondmen tremble. Must I budge?
45 Must I observe you? Must I stand and crouch
46 Under your testy humor? By the gods,

25 the mighty . . . honors our great power to confer honorable public offices
26 trash money (contemptuous) 27 bay howl at 28 bait harass 30
hedge me in i.e. limit my authority 32 make conditions manage affairs 35
Urge drive 36 health safety; Tempt provoke 37 slight worthless 39
way . . . choler course and scope to your rash anger 40 stares glares 44
budge flinch 45 observe wait upon obsequiously; crouch bow 46 testy
humor irritable temper

You shall digest the venom of your spleen,   47
Though it do split you ; for from this day forth
I'll use you for my mirth, yea, for my laughter,   49
When you are waspish.

CASSIUS   Is it come to this ?

BRUTUS
You say you are a better soldier.
Let it appear so ; make your vaunting true,   52
And it shall please me well. For mine own part,
I shall be glad to learn of noble men.   54

CASSIUS
You wrong me every way ! You wrong me, Brutus !
I said an elder soldier, not a better.
Did I say 'better' ?

BRUTUS   If you did, I care not.

CASSIUS
When Caesar lived he durst not thus have moved me.   58

BRUTUS
Peace, peace ! You durst not so have tempted him.   59

CASSIUS I durst not ?

BRUTUS No.

CASSIUS
What, durst not tempt him ?

BRUTUS   For your life you durst not.

CASSIUS
Do not presume too much upon my love.
I may do that I shall be sorry for.

BRUTUS
You have done that you should be sorry for.
There is no terror, Cassius, in your threats ;
For I am armed so strong in honesty   67
That they pass by me as the idle wind,

---

47 *digest the venom* swallow the poison; *spleen* i.e. hot temper   49 *laughter*
object of ridicule   52 *vaunting* boasting   54 *learn of* hear of the existence
of (with pun on 'take lessons from')   58 *moved* angered   59 *tempted*
provoked   67 *honesty* integrity

69   Which I respect not. I did send to you
        For certain sums of gold, which you denied me ;
        For I can raise no money by vile means.
        By heaven, I had rather coin my heart
        And drop my blood for drachmas than to wring
        From the hard hands of peasants their vile trash
75   By any indirection. I did send
        To you for gold to pay my legions,
        Which you denied me. Was that done like Cassius ?
        Should I have answered Caius Cassius so ?
        When Marcus Brutus grows so covetous
80   To lock such rascal counters from his friends,
        Be ready, gods, with all your thunderbolts,
        Dash him to pieces !

CASSIUS   I denied you not.
BRUTUS You did.
CASSIUS
        I did not. He was but a fool that brought
85   My answer back. Brutus hath rived my heart.
        A friend should bear his friend's infirmities,
        But Brutus makes mine greater than they are.
BRUTUS
        I do not, till you practise them on me.
CASSIUS
        You love me not.
BRUTUS   I do not like your faults.
CASSIUS
        A friendly eye could never see such faults.
BRUTUS
        A flatterer's would not, though they do appear
        As huge as high Olympus.
CASSIUS
        Come, Antony, and young Octavius, come !
94   Revenge yourselves alone on Cassius.

69 *respect not* ignore   75 *indirection* irregular means   80 *rascal counters*
base coins   85 *rived* split in two   94 *alone* solely

104

For Cassius is aweary of the world :
Hated by one he loves ; braved by his brother ;   96
Checked like a bondman ; all his faults observed,   97
Set in a notebook, learned and conned by rote
To cast into my teeth. O, I could weep   99
My spirit from mine eyes ! There is my dagger,
And here my naked breast ; within, a heart
Dearer than Pluto's mine, richer than gold.   102
If that thou be'st a Roman, take it forth.
I, that denied thee gold, will give my heart.
Strike as thou didst at Caesar ; for I know,
When thou didst hate him worst, thou lovedst him better
Than ever thou lovedst Cassius.

BRUTUS   Sheathe your dagger.
Be angry when you will ; it shall have scope.   108
Do what you will ; dishonor shall be humor.   109
O Cassius, you are yokèd with a lamb
That carries anger as the flint bears fire ;
Who, much enforcèd, shows a hasty spark,   112
And straight is cold again.   113

CASSIUS   Hath Cassius lived
To be but mirth and laughter to his Brutus
When grief and blood ill-tempered vexeth him ?   115

BRUTUS
When I spoke that, I was ill-tempered too.

CASSIUS
Do you confess so much ? Give me your hand.

BRUTUS
And my heart too.

CASSIUS   O Brutus !

BRUTUS   What's the matter ?

---

96 *braved* defied   97 *Checked* scolded   99 *cast . . . teeth* i.e. throw up to me
102 *Dearer . . . mine* more precious than the riches within the earth (Pluto,
god of the underworld, probably confused with Plutus, god of riches)
108 *it* i.e. your anger; *scope* free play   109 *dishonor . . . humor* I shall take
your insults as an effect of your hot temper   112 *enforcèd* worked upon
113 *straight* at once   115 *blood ill-tempered* unbalanced disposition

CASSIUS
Have you not love enough to bear with me
120   When that rash humor which my mother gave me
Makes me forgetful ?

BRUTUS   Yes, Cassius ; and from henceforth,
When you are over-earnest with your Brutus,
123   He'll think your mother chides, and leave you so.
        *Enter a Poet [followed by Lucilius, Titinius, and
        Lucius].*

POET
Let me go in to see the generals !
125   There is some grudge between 'em. 'Tis not meet
They be alone.

LUCILIUS   You shall not come to them.

POET
Nothing but death shall stay me.

CASSIUS   How now ? What's the matter ?

POET
For shame, you generals ! What do you mean ?
Love and be friends, as two such men should be ;
For I have seen more years, I'm sure, than ye.

CASSIUS
133   Ha, ha ! How vilely doth this cynic rhyme !

BRUTUS
134   Get you hence, sirrah ! Saucy fellow, hence !

CASSIUS
Bear with him, Brutus. 'Tis his fashion.

BRUTUS
136   I'll know his humor when he knows his time.
137   What should the wars do with these jigging fools ?
138   Companion, hence !

CASSIUS   Away, away, be gone !   *Exit Poet.*

120 *rash humor* choleric or splenetic temperament   123 *mother* i.e. inherited temperament (also hysteria?); *leave you so* leave it at that   125 *grudge* ill-feeling   133 *cynic* boorish fellow   134 *sirrah* (contemptuous form of address); *Saucy* insolent   136 *I'll . . . time* I'll accept his fashion of behavior when he knows the proper time and place for it   137 *jigging* rhyming (contemptuous), doggerel versifying   138 *Companion* fellow (contemptuous)

BRUTUS
Lucilius and Titinius, bid the commanders
Prepare to lodge their companies to-night.

CASSIUS
And come yourselves, and bring Messala with you
Immediately to us.   *[Exeunt Lucilius and Titinius.]*

BRUTUS   Lucius, a bowl of wine. *[Exit Lucius.]*

CASSIUS
I did not think you could have been so angry.

BRUTUS
O Cassius, I am sick of many griefs.

CASSIUS
Of your philosophy you make no use
If you give place to accidental evils.   146

BRUTUS
No man bears sorrow better. Portia is dead.

CASSIUS Ha! Portia?

BRUTUS She is dead.

CASSIUS
How scaped I killing when I crossed you so?   150
O insupportable and touching loss!   151
Upon what sickness?   152

BRUTUS   Impatient of my absence,
And grief that young Octavius with Mark Antony
Have made themselves so strong; for with her death   154
That tidings came. With this she fell distract,   155
And (her attendants absent) swallowed fire.   156

CASSIUS
And died so?

---

146 *place* way; *accidental evils* evils caused by chance (i.e. Brutus, as a Stoic, should not be affected by those external adversities caused by Fortune) 150 *killing* being killed by you; *crossed* opposed   151 *touching* grievous 152 *Upon* as a result of; *Impatient of* unable to endure (also desperate at?) 154-55 *for . . . came* for together with the news of her death came the news of their strength   155 *distract* distraught   156 *swallowed fire* (according to Plutarch, as translated by North, she cast 'hot burning coals [from a charcoal brazier] . . . into her mouth, and kept her mouth so close that she choked herself')

BRUTUS   Even so.
CASSIUS   O ye immortal gods!

Enter Boy [Lucius], with wine and tapers.

BRUTUS
Speak no more of her. Give me a bowl of wine.
159   In this I bury all unkindness, Cassius.

Drinks.

CASSIUS
My heart is thirsty for that noble pledge.
Fill, Lucius, till the wine o'erswell the cup.
I cannot drink too much of Brutus' love.

                         [Drinks. Exit Lucius.]

Enter Titinius and Messala.

BRUTUS
Come in, Titinius! Welcome, good Messala.
Now sit we close about this taper here
165   And call in question our necessities.

CASSIUS
Portia, art thou gone?

BRUTUS   No more, I pray you.
Messala, I have here receivèd letters
That young Octavius and Mark Antony
169   Come down upon us with a mighty power,
170   Bending their expedition toward Philippi.

MESSALA
171   Myself have letters of the selfsame tenure.

BRUTUS
With what addition?

MESSALA
173   That by proscription and bills of outlawry
Octavius, Antony, and Lepidus
Have put to death an hundred senators.

---

159 *In . . . unkindness* in this wine I'll drown all our differences   165 *call in question* deliberate upon   169 *upon* against; *power* army   170 *Bending* directing; *expedition* rapid march   171 *tenure* tenor, purport   173 *proscription* condemnation to death; *bills of outlawry* proscription lists

BRUTUS
Therein our letters do not well agree.
Mine speak of seventy senators that died
By their proscriptions, Cicero being one.

CASSIUS
Cicero one?

MESSALA   Cicero is dead,
And by that order of proscription.
Had you your letters from your wife, my lord?   181

BRUTUS No, Messala.

MESSALA
Nor nothing in your letters writ of her?

BRUTUS
Nothing, Messala.

MESSALA   That methinks is strange.

BRUTUS
Why ask you? Hear you aught of her in yours?

MESSALA No, my lord.

BRUTUS
Now as you are a Roman, tell me true.

MESSALA
Then like a Roman bear the truth I tell;
For certain she is dead, and by strange manner.

BRUTUS
Why, farewell, Portia. We must die, Messala.
With meditating that she must die once,   191
I have the patience to endure it now.

MESSALA
Even so great men great losses should endure.

CASSIUS
I have as much of this in art as you,   194
But yet my nature could not bear it so.   195

181–95 (some editors, assuming revision, bracket or delete this episode as contradictory and redundant of ll. 143–58 and 166) 191 *once* at some time 194 *this in art* i.e. this stoical fortitude in philosophical theory 195 *nature* natural emotions

BRUTUS

196   Well, to our work alive. What do you think
      Of marching to Philippi presently?

CASSIUS

      I do not think it good.

BRUTUS   Your reason?

CASSIUS   This it is:

      'Tis better that the enemy seek us.
      So shall he waste his means, weary his soldiers,
201   Doing himself offense, whilst we, lying still,
      Are full of rest, defense, and nimbleness.

BRUTUS

203   Good reasons must of force give place to better.
      The people 'twixt Philippi and this ground
205   Do stand but in a forced affection;
      For they have grudged us contribution.
      The enemy, marching along by them,
      By them shall make a fuller number up,
209   Come on refreshed, new added, and encouraged;
      From which advantage shall we cut him off
      If at Philippi we do face him there,
      These people at our back.

CASSIUS   Hear me, good brother.

BRUTUS

      Under your pardon. You must note beside
      That we have tried the utmost of our friends,
      Our legions are brimful, our cause is ripe.
      The enemy increaseth every day;
      We, at the height, are ready to decline.
      There is a tide in the affairs of men
      Which, taken at the flood, leads on to fortune;
220   Omitted, all the voyage of their life
221   Is bound in shallows and in miseries.

---

196 *alive* that concerns us as living men   201 *offense* injury   203 *of force* of necessity   205 *Do . . . affection* favor us only by compulsion   209 *new added* reinforced   220 *Omitted* not taken   221 *bound in* confined to

On such a full sea are we now afloat,
And we must take the current when it serves
Or lose our ventures.   224

CASSIUS   Then, with your will, go on.
We'll along ourselves and meet them at Philippi.

BRUTUS
The deep of night is crept upon our talk
And nature must obey necessity,
Which we will niggard with a little rest.   228
There is no more to say?

CASSIUS   No more. Good night.
Early to-morrow will we rise and hence.   230

BRUTUS
Lucius! *(Enter Lucius.)* My gown.   *[Exit Lucius.]* 231
                        Farewell, good Messala.
Good night, Titinius. Noble, noble Cassius,
Good night and good repose.

CASSIUS   O my dear brother,
This was an ill beginning of the night!
Never come such division 'tween our souls!
Let it not, Brutus.
            Enter Lucius, with the gown.

BRUTUS   Everything is well.

CASSIUS
Good night, my lord.

BRUTUS   Good night, good brother.

TITINIUS, MESSALA
Good night, Lord Brutus.

BRUTUS   Farewell every one.
            Exeunt [Cassius, Titinius, and Messala].
Give me the gown. Where is thy instrument?   239

LUCIUS
Here in the tent.

---

224 *ventures* investments risked on the high seas; *with your will* as you wish
228 *niggard* stint, i.e. sleep only a short time   230 *hence* go from here   231
gown dressing gown   239 *instrument* lute or cithern

NICE TO SOLDIERS

BRUTUS   What, thou speak'st drowsily?
241   Poor knave, I blame thee not; thou art o'erwatched.
       Call Claudius and some other of my men;
       I'll have them sleep on cushions in my tent.
LUCIUS Varro and Claudius!
              Enter Varro and Claudius.
VARRO   Calls my lord?
BRUTUS
       I pray you, sirs, lie in my tent and sleep.
247   It may be I shall raise you by and by
       On business to my brother Cassius.
VARRO
249   So please you, we will stand and watch your pleasure.
BRUTUS
       I will not have it so. Lie down, good sirs.
251   It may be I shall otherwise bethink me.
              [Varro and Claudius lie down.]
       Look, Lucius, here's the book I sought for so;
       I put it in the pocket of my gown.
LUCIUS
       I was sure your lordship did not give it me.
BRUTUS
       Bear with me, good boy, I am much forgetful.
       Canst thou hold up thy heavy eyes awhile,
257   And touch thy instrument a strain or two?
LUCIUS
258   Ay, my lord, an't please you.
BRUTUS   It does, my boy.
       I trouble thee too much, but thou art willing.
LUCIUS It is my duty, sir.
BRUTUS
       I should not urge thy duty past thy might.
262   I know young bloods look for a time of rest.

---

241 *knave* lad (affectionate); *o'erwatched* tired from lack of sleep   247 *raise*
rouse; *by and by* soon   249 *watch your pleasure* await your commands   251
otherwise bethink me change my mind   257 *touch* play on; *strain* musical
composition   258 *an't* if it   262 *young bloods* youthful constitutions

LUCIUS I have slept, my lord, already.

BRUTUS

It was well done ; and thou shalt sleep again ;
I will not hold thee long. If I do live,   265
I will be good to thee.   266
    Music, and a song. [Lucius falls asleep.]
This is a sleepy tune. O murd'rous slumber !   267
Layest thou thy leaden mace upon my boy,   268
That plays thee music ? Gentle knave, good night.
I will not do thee so much wrong to wake thee.
If thou dost nod, thou break'st thy instrument ;
I'll take it from thee ; and, good boy, good night.
Let me see, let me see. Is not the leaf turned down *NO BOOKS*
Where I left reading ? Here it is, I think.
    [Sits.] Enter the Ghost of Caesar.
How ill this taper burns ! Ha, who comes here ?   275
I think it is the weakness of mine eyes   *GUILT*   276
That shapes this monstrous apparition.   *OVER*
It comes upon me. Art thou any thing ?   *KILLING*   278
Art thou some god, some angel, or some devil, *CAESAR*
That mak'st my blood cold and my hair to stare ?   280
Speak to me what thou art.

GHOST

Thy evil spirit, Brutus.

BRUTUS   Why com'st thou ?

GHOST

To tell thee thou shalt see me at Philippi.

BRUTUS Well ; then I shall see thee again ?

GHOST Ay, at Philippi.

---

265 *hold* detain **266** s.d. *Music, and a song* (stage tradition prescribes the use of 'Orpheus with his lute,' from *Henry VIII*; more appropriate is 'Come, heavy sleep,' from John Dowland's *First Book of Songs*, 1597) **267** *murd'rous* giving the appearance of death **268** *leaden* heavy (lead was associated with death); *mace* staff of office with which a man was touched on the shoulder when arrested **275** *How . . . burns* (it was commonly held that lights burned dim or blue in the presence of a ghost or spirit) **276** *weakness . . . eyes* i.e. possibly a hallucination **278** *upon* toward **280** *stare* stand on end

BRUTUS
Why, I will see thee at Philippi then.   *[Exit Ghost.]*
Now I have taken heart thou vanishest.
Ill spirit, I would hold more talk with thee.
Boy. Lucius! Varro, Claudius. Sirs! Awake!
Claudius!

291 LUCIUS The strings, my lord, are false.

BRUTUS
He thinks he still is at his instrument.
Lucius, awake!

LUCIUS My lord?

BRUTUS
Didst thou dream, Lucius, that thou so criedst out?

LUCIUS
My lord, I do not know that I did cry.

BRUTUS
Yes, that thou didst. Didst thou see anything?

LUCIUS Nothing, my lord.

BRUTUS
Sleep again, Lucius. Sirrah Claudius!
        [To Varro]
Fellow thou, awake!

VARRO My lord?

CLAUDIUS My lord?

BRUTUS
Why did you so cry out, sirs, in your sleep?

BOTH
Did we, my lord?

BRUTUS   Ay. Saw you anything?

VARRO
No, my lord, I saw nothing.

CLAUDIUS   Nor I, my lord.

BRUTUS
306 Go and commend me to my brother Cassius.

291 *false* out of tune   306 *commend me* give my greetings

Bid him set on his pow'rs betimes before,   307
And we will follow.

BOTH   It shall be done, my lord.   *Exeunt.*

*

    Enter Octavius, Antony, and their Army.   V, i

OCTAVIUS
Now, Antony, our hopes are answerèd.
You said the enemy would not come down
But keep the hills and upper regions.
It proves not so. Their battles are at hand;   4
They mean to warn us at Philippi here,   5
Answering before we do demand of them.   6

ANTONY
Tut! I am in their bosoms and I know   7
Wherefore they do it. They could be content   8
To visit other places, and come down
With fearful bravery, thinking by this face   10
To fasten in our thoughts that they have courage.   11
But 'tis not so.
    Enter a Messenger.

MESSENGER   Prepare you, generals.
The enemy comes on in gallant show;   13
Their bloody sign of battle is hung out,   14
And something to be done immediately.

ANTONY
Octavius, lead your battle softly on   16
Upon the left hand of the even field.

307 *set on* advance; *betimes before* early in the morning before me
V, i The plains of Philippi   **4** *proves* turns out to be; *battles* armies   **5**
warn challenge   **6** *Answering . . . them* appearing against us before we call
them to combat   **7** *in their bosoms* aware of their secrets (i.e. he has spies in
their army)   **8–9** *could . . . places* would prefer to be elsewhere   **10** *fearful*
bravery display that inspires (with pun on 'is full of') fear; *face* show   **11**
fasten fix the idea   **13** *gallant* splendid   **14** *bloody sign* red flag   **16** *battle*
army; *softly* slowly

OCTAVIUS
Upon the right hand I. Keep thou the left.

ANTONY

19   Why do you cross me in this exigent?

OCTAVIUS
I do not cross you; but I will do so.

March. Drum. Enter Brutus, Cassius, and their Army
[; Lucilius, Titinius, Messala, and others].

BRUTUS
They stand and would have parley.

CASSIUS
Stand fast, Titinius. We must out and talk.

OCTAVIUS
Mark Antony, shall we give sign of battle?

ANTONY

24   No, Caesar, we will answer on their charge.

25   Make forth. The generals would have some words.

OCTAVIUS
Stir not until the signal.

BRUTUS
Words before blows. Is it so, countrymen?

OCTAVIUS
Not that we love words better, as you do.

BRUTUS
Good words are better than bad strokes, Octavius.

ANTONY
In your bad strokes, Brutus, you give good words;
Witness the hole you made in Caesar's heart,
Crying 'Long live! Hail, Caesar!'

CASSIUS   Antony,

33   The posture of your blows are yet unknown;

34   But for your words, they rob the Hybla bees,
And leave them honeyless.

ANTONY   Not stingless too.

---

19 *cross* oppose; *exigent* critical moment **24** *on their charge* when they attack **25** *Make forth* go forward **33** *posture* fashion, quality **34** *Hybla* a Sicilian town famous for the sweetness of its honey

BRUTUS
O yes, and soundless too!
For you have stol'n their buzzing, Antony,
And very wisely threat before you sting.

ANTONY
Villains! you did not so when your vile daggers   39
Hacked one another in the sides of Caesar.
You showed your teeth like apes, and fawned like hounds, 41
And bowed like bondmen, kissing Caesar's feet;
Whilst damnèd Casca, like a cur, behind
Struck Caesar on the neck. O you flatterers!

CASSIUS
Flatterers? Now, Brutus, thank yourself!
This tongue had not offended so to-day
If Cassius might have ruled.   47

OCTAVIUS
Come, come, the cause! If arguing make us sweat,   48
The proof of it will turn to redder drops.   49
Look,
I draw a sword against conspirators.
When think you that the sword goes up again?   52
Never, till Caesar's three-and-thirty wounds
Be well avenged, or till another Caesar   54
Have added slaughter to the sword of traitors.   55

BRUTUS
Caesar, thou canst not die by traitors' hands
Unless thou bring'st them with thee.

OCTAVIUS   So I hope.
I was not born to die on Brutus' sword.

BRUTUS
O, if thou wert the noblest of thy strain,   59
Young man, thou couldst not die more honorable.

39 *so* i.e. give warning   **41** *showed your teeth* grinned obsequiously   **47** *ruled* had his way (at II, i, 155–61)   **48** *the cause* to our business   **49** *proof* trial   **52** *goes up* will be sheathed   **54** *another Caesar* i.e. himself   **55** *Have …to* has also been killed by   **59** *strain* line of descent

CASSIUS

61 A peevish schoolboy, worthless of such honor,
62 Joined with a masker and a reveller!

ANTONY
Old Cassius still.

OCTAVIUS   Come, Antony. Away!
Defiance, traitors, hurl we in your teeth.
If you dare fight to-day, come to the field;
66 If not, when you have stomachs.

Exit Octavius, [with] Antony, and Army.

CASSIUS
Why, now blow wind, swell billow, and swim bark!
68 The storm is up, and all is on the hazard.

BRUTUS
Ho, Lucilius! Hark, a word with you.
Lucilius stands forth.

LUCILIUS   My lord?
[Brutus and Lucilius converse apart.]

CASSIUS
Messala.
Messala stands forth.

MESSALA   What says my general?

CASSIUS   Messala,
This is my birthday; as this very day
Was Cassius born. Give me thy hand, Messala.
Be thou my witness that against my will
74 (As Pompey was) am I compelled to set
Upon one battle all our liberties.
76 You know that I held Epicurus strong
And his opinion. Now I change my mind
78 And partly credit things that do presage.

61 *peevish* childish (Octavius was twenty-one); *worthless* unworthy **62** *masker . . . reveller* (see II, i, 189; II, ii, 116) **66** *stomachs* appetite (for battle) **68** *on the hazard* at stake **74** *As Pompey was* (at Pharsalus, where he was persuaded to give battle to Caesar against his will; see I, i, 37n.); *set* stake, gamble **76–77** *held . . . opinion* was a convinced follower of the Epicurean philosophy, i.e. a materialist, who thought it foolishly superstitious to believe in omens (cf. II, i, 193–201) **78** *credit* believe in

Coming from Sardis, on our former ensign 79
Two mighty eagles fell; and there they perched, 80
Gorging and feeding from our soldiers' hands,
Who to Philippi here consorted us. 82
This morning are they fled away and gone,
And in their steads do ravens, crows, and kites 84
Fly o'er our heads and downward look on us
As we were sickly prey. Their shadows seem 86
A canopy most fatal, under which 87
Our army lies, ready to give up the ghost.

MESSALA
Believe not so.

CASSIUS   I but believe it partly; 89
For I am fresh of spirit and resolved
To meet all perils very constantly. 91

BRUTUS
Even so, Lucilius.

CASSIUS   Now, most noble Brutus,
The gods to-day stand friendly, that we may, 93
Lovers in peace, lead on our days to age! 94
But since the affairs of men rests still incertain, 95
Let's reason with the worst that may befall. 96
If we do lose this battle, then is this
The very last time we shall speak together.
What are you then determinèd to do? 99

BRUTUS
Even by the rule of that philosophy 100
By which I did blame Cato for the death 101
Which he did give himself – I know not how,
But I do find it cowardly and vile,

---

79 *former* foremost; *ensign* standard, banner   80 *fell* swooped down   82
consorted accompanied   84 *ravens . . . kites* scavengers which proverbially
anticipate death   86 *sickly* dying   87 *fatal* foreboding death   89 *but* only
91 *constantly* resolutely   93 *The . . . friendly* may the gods be well-disposed
toward us to-day   94 *Lovers* dear friends   95 *rests still* remain always   96
reason . . . befall consider what to do if the worst should happen   99 *then*
i.e. if we should lose   100 *that philosophy* i.e. Stoicism   101 *Cato* (see II,
i, 295n.)

104   For fear of what might fall, so to prevent
105   The time of life – arming myself with patience
106   To stay the providence of some high powers
       That govern us below.

CASSIUS   Then, if we lose this battle,
108   You are contented to be led in triumph
       Thorough the streets of Rome.

BRUTUS
       No, Cassius, no. Think not, thou noble Roman,
111   That ever Brutus will go bound to Rome.
       He bears too great a mind. But this same day
       Must end that work the ides of March begun,
       And whether we shall meet again I know not.
       Therefore our everlasting farewell take.
       For ever and for ever farewell, Cassius !
       If we do meet again, why, we shall smile ;
       If not, why then this parting was well made.

CASSIUS
       For ever and for ever farewell, Brutus !
       If we do meet again, we'll smile indeed ;
       If not, 'tis true this parting was well made.

BRUTUS
       Why then, lead on. O that a man might know
       The end of this day's business ere it come !
       But it sufficeth that the day will end,
       And then the end is known. Come, ho ! Away !   *Exeunt.*

V, ii   *Alarum. Enter Brutus and Messala.*

BRUTUS
1   Ride, ride, Messala, ride, and give these bills
2   Unto the legions on the other side.

---

104 *fall* happen; *prevent* anticipate   105 *time* natural limit   106 *stay* wait
for; *providence* destiny; *some* whatever (i.e. Brutus does not believe in the
Roman gods, but he does believe in 'powers' whose nature he cannot
exactly define)   108 *in triumph* in a victory procession (as a captive)   111
bound in chains (as a captive)
V, ii   s.d. *Alarum* a drum signal calling to arms   1 *bills* written orders
2 *side* wing (of the army), i.e. Cassius' forces

Loud alarum.

Let them set on at once; for I perceive   3
But cold demeanor in Octavius' wing,   4
And sudden push gives them the overthrow.   5
Ride, ride, Messala! Let them all come down.   6

                                    Exeunt.

Alarums. Enter Cassius and Titinius.   V, iii

CASSIUS
O, look, Titinius, look! The villains fly!   1
Myself have to mine own turned enemy.   2
This ensign here of mine was turning back;   3
I slew the coward and did take it from him.   4

TITINIUS
O Cassius, Brutus gave the word too early,
Who, having some advantage on Octavius,   6
Took it too eagerly. His soldiers fell to spoil, 7
Whilst we by Antony are all enclosed.

Enter Pindarus.

PINDARUS
Fly further off, my lord! fly further off!
Mark Antony is in your tents, my lord.   10
Fly, therefore, noble Cassius, fly far off!   11

CASSIUS
This hill is far enough. Look, look, Titinius!
Are those my tents where I perceive the fire?

TITINIUS
They are, my lord.

CASSIUS   Titinius, if thou lovest me,
Mount thou my horse and hide thy spurs in him
Till he have brought thee up to yonder troops
And here again, that I may rest assured
Whether yond troops are friend or enemy.

---

3 *set on* attack **4** *cold demeanor* lack of spirit (in battle) **5** *push* assault;
gives...overthrow will defeat them **6** *them...down* the whole army attack
V, iii **1** *villains* i.e. his own troops **2** *mine own* my own men **3** *ensign*
standard-bearer **4** *it* i.e. the standard he was bearing **6** *on* over **7** *spoil*
looting **10** *tents* encampment **11** *far* farther

TITINIUS
19   I will be here again even with a thought.   *Exit.*

CASSIUS
      Go, Pindarus, get higher on that hill.
21   My sight was ever thick. Regard Titinius,
22   And tell me what thou not'st about the field.
            [Pindarus goes up.]
      This day I breathèd first. Time is come round,
      And where I did begin, there shall I end.
25   My life is run his compass. Sirrah, what news?
26 PINDARUS *(above)* O my lord!

CASSIUS What news?

PINDARUS *[above]*
      Titinius is enclosèd round about
29   With horsemen that make to him on the spur.
      Yet he spurs on. Now they are almost on him.
31   Now Titinius. Now some light. O, he lights too!
32   He's ta'en. *(Shout.)* And hark! They shout for joy.

CASSIUS
      Come down; behold no more.
      O coward that I am to live so long
      To see my best friend ta'en before my face!
            Enter Pindarus [from above].
      Come hither, sirrah.
      In Parthia did I take thee prisoner;
38   And then I swore thee, saving of thy life,
      That whatsoever I did bid thee do,
      Thou shouldst attempt it. Come now, keep thine oath.
      Now be a freeman, and with this good sword,
42   That ran through Caesar's bowels, search this bosom.
43   Stand not to answer. Here, take thou the hilts;

---

19 *even ... thought* in the twinkling of an eye   21 *thick* dim, i.e. near-sighted;
Regard observe   22 *not'st* observe   25 *is ... compass* has completed its full
circuit   26 s.d. *above* (on the 'upper stage')   29 *make to* approach; *on the
spur* rapidly   31 *light* dismount   32 *ta'en* captured   38 *swore thee* made
you swear; *saving of* when I spared   42 *search* probe, penetrate into   43
Stand delay

And when my face is covered, as 'tis now,
Guide thou the sword.
  [Pindarus stabs him.] Caesar, thou art revenged
Even with the sword that killed thee.
  [Dies.]

PINDARUS
 So, I am free ; yet would not so have been,   47
 Durst I have done my will. O Cassius !   48
 Far from this country Pindarus shall run,
 Where never Roman shall take note of him. *[Exit.]*
  Enter Titinius and Messala.

MESSALA
 It is but change, Titinius ; for Octavius   51
 Is overthrown by noble Brutus' power,
 As Cassius' legions are by Antony.

TITINIUS
 These tidings will well comfort Cassius.   54

MESSALA
 Where did you leave him ?

TITINIUS   All disconsolate,
 With Pindarus his bondman, on this hill.

MESSALA
 Is not that he that lies upon the ground ?

TITINIUS
 He lies not like the living. O my heart !

MESSALA
 Is not that he ?

TITINIUS   No, this was he, Messala,
 But Cassius is no more. O setting sun,   60
 As in thy red rays thou dost sink to night,
 So in his red blood Cassius' day is set !
 The sun of Rome is set. Our day is gone ;

---

47 *not so* not in such circumstances **48** *my will* (rather than Cassius' will,
which he was sworn to do) **51** *change* an exchange, '*quid pro quo*' **54** *comfort* encourage **60** *setting sun* (a figurative comparison: actually it is mid-afternoon – see l. 109)

64   Clouds, dews, and dangers come ; our deeds are done !
65   ~~Mistrust of my success hath done this deed.~~

MESSALA
      Mistrust of good success hath done this deed.
67   O hateful Error, Melancholy's child,   *FEAR OF UNREAL*
68   Why dost thou show to the apt thoughts of men
      The things that are not ? O Error, soon conceived,
      Thou never com'st unto a happy birth,
71   But kill'st the mother that engend'red thee !

TITINIUS
      What, Pindarus ! Where art thou, Pindarus ?

MESSALA
      Seek him, Titinius, whilst I go to meet
      The noble Brutus, thrusting this report
      Into his ears. I may say 'thrusting' it ;
      For piercing steel and darts envenomèd
      Shall be as welcome to the ears of Brutus
      As tidings of this sight.

78 TITINIUS   Hie you, Messala,
      And I will seek for Pindarus the while.   *[Exit Messala.]*
80   Why didst thou send me forth, brave Cassius ?
      Did I not meet thy friends, and did not they
      Put on my brows this wreath of victory
      And bid me give it thee ? Didst thou not hear their
          shouts ?
84   Alas, thou hast misconstrued everything !
85   But hold thee, take this garland on thy brow.
      Thy Brutus bid me give it thee, and I
      Will do his bidding. Brutus, come apace
88   And see how I regarded Caius Cassius.
89   By your leave, gods. This is a Roman's part.

---

64 *dews* (see II, i, 262n., 265n.) **65** *Mistrust...success* fear as to how I should
make out **67** *Melancholy's child* (melancholy persons fear unreal dangers)
68 *apt* impressionable **71** *mother* i.e. the melancholy person who conceived
the error **78** *Hie* hurry **80** *brave* noble **84** *misconstrued* (accented on
second syllable) **85** *hold thee* wait a minute **88** *regarded* respected,
honored **89** *leave* permission; *part* role, function (in such circumstances)

Come, Cassius' sword, and find Titinius' heart.

Dies.

*Alarum. Enter Brutus, Messala, Young Cato,
Strato, Volumnius, and Lucilius.*

BRUTUS

Where, where, Messala, doth his body lie?

MESSALA

Lo, yonder, and Titinius mourning it.

BRUTUS

Titinius' face is upward.

CATO   He is slain.

BRUTUS

O Julius Caesar, thou art mighty yet!
Thy spirit walks abroad and turns our swords
In our own proper entrails.   96

Low alarums.

CATO   Brave Titinius!

Look whe'r he have not crowned dead Cassius.

BRUTUS

Are yet two Romans living such as these?
The last of all the Romans, fare thee well!
It is impossible that ever Rome
Should breed thy fellow. Friends, I owe moe tears   101
To this dead man than you shall see me pay.
I shall find time, Cassius; I shall find time.
Come therefore, and to Thasos send his body.   104
His funerals shall not be in our camp,
Lest it discomfort us. Lucilius, come;   106
And come, young Cato. Let us to the field.
Labeo and Flavius set our battles on.   108
'Tis three o'clock; and, Romans, yet ere night
We shall try fortune in a second fight.

                                        Exeunt.

---

96 *own proper* very own; *Brave* noble   101 *moe* more   104 *Thasos* an island
near Philippi where, according to Plutarch, Cassius was buried   106
discomfort us dishearten our army   108 *battles* forces

V, iv   *Alarum. Enter Brutus, Messala, [Young] Cato,*
               Lucilius, and Flavius.

BRUTUS
   Yet, countrymen, O, yet hold up your heads!
                    [Exit, followed by Messala and Flavius.]

CATO
2   What bastard doth not? Who will go with me?
     I will proclaim my name about the field.
4   I am the son of Marcus Cato, ho!
5   A foe to tyrants, and my country's friend.
     I am the son of Marcus Cato, ho!
         Enter Soldiers and fight.

LUCILIUS
7   And I am Brutus, Marcus Brutus I!
     Brutus, my country's friend! Know me for Brutus!
             [Young Cato falls.]
     O young and noble Cato, art thou down?
10   Why, now thou diest as bravely as Titinius,
     And mayst be honored, being Cato's son.

[1.] SOLDIER
   Yield, or thou diest.

12 LUCILIUS   Only I yield to die.
13   There is so much that thou wilt kill me straight.
     Kill Brutus, and be honored in his death.

[1.] SOLDIER
   We must not. A noble prisoner!
         Enter Antony.

2. SOLDIER
   Room ho! Tell Antony Brutus is ta'en.

V, iv   2 *What bastard* who is so low-born that he   4 *Cato* (see II, i, 295n.)
5 *tyrants* (such as Caesar and his followers)   7 *Lucilius* (in the folio this
speech-prefix appears at l. 9, but Lucilius, as indicated in Plutarch, also
speaks ll. 7–8, impersonating Brutus, though some editors give ll. 7–8 to
Brutus)   10 *bravely* nobly   12 *Only ... die* I surrender only in order to die
13 *so much* so great an inducement to honor and fame (?), so much that I can
be blamed for (?) (some editors suppose an offer of money); *straight* at
once

1. SOLDIER
  I'll tell the news. Here comes the general.
  Brutus is ta'en! Brutus is ta'en, my lord!

ANTONY Where is he?

LUCILIUS
  Safe, Antony; Brutus is safe enough.
  I dare assure thee that no enemy
  Shall ever take alive the noble Brutus.
  The gods defend him from so great a shame!
  When you do find him, or alive or dead,
  He will be found like Brutus, like himself.   25

ANTONY
  This is not Brutus, friend; but, I assure you,
  A prize no less in worth. Keep this man safe;
  Give him all kindness. I had rather have
  Such men my friends than enemies. Go on,
  And see whe'r Brutus be alive or dead;
  And bring us word unto Octavius' tent
  How every thing is chanced.   32

                                                    Exeunt.

        Enter Brutus, Dardanius, Clitus, Strato,   V, v
        and Volumnius.

BRUTUS
  Come, poor remains of friends, rest on this rock.   1

CLITUS
  Statilius showed the torchlight; but, my lord,   2
  He came not back. He is or ta'en or slain.

BRUTUS
  Sit thee down, Clitus. Slaying is the word.
  It is a deed in fashion. Hark thee, Clitus.
      [Whispers.]

CLITUS
  What, I, my lord? No, not for all the world!

---

25 *like himself* true to his noble nature   **32** *is chanced* has happened
V, v 1 *poor remains* pitiful survivors   **2** *Statilius . . . torchlight* i.e. a
scout who got as far as Cassius' encampment, occupied by Antony's
troops, from which he signalled

BRUTUS
Peace then. No words.

CLITUS   I'll rather kill myself.

BRUTUS
Hark thee, Dardanius.
    [*Whispers.*]

DARDANIUS   Shall I do such a deed?

CLITUS O Dardanius!

DARDANIUS O Clitus!

CLITUS
What ill request did Brutus make to thee?

DARDANIUS
To kill him, Clitus. Look, he meditates.

CLITUS
13 Now is that noble vessel full of grief,
That it runs over even at his eyes.

BRUTUS
Come hither, good Volumnius. List a word.

VOLUMNIUS
What says my lord?

BRUTUS   Why this, Volumnius.
The ghost of Caesar hath appeared to me
18 Two several times by night – at Sardis once,
And this last night here in Philippi fields.
I know my hour is come.

VOLUMNIUS   Not so, my lord.

BRUTUS
Nay, I am sure it is, Volumnius.
Thou seest the world, Volumnius, how it goes.
23 Our enemies have beat us to the pit.
        Low alarums.
24 It is more worthy to leap in ourselves
Than tarry till they push us. Good Volumnius,

---

13 *noble vessel* completely noble man (also a sacred vessel for holding the
tears of devout mourners)   18 *several* different   23 *the pit* (into which a
wild animal is driven in order to be captured; with pun on 'the grave')   24
more worthy nobler

JULIUS CAESAR

    Thou know'st that we two went to school together.
    Even for that our love of old, I prithee
    Hold thou my sword-hilts whilst I run on it.

VOLUMNIUS
    That's not an office for a friend, my lord.
        Alarum still.

CLITUS
    Fly, fly, my lord! There is no tarrying here.

BRUTUS
    Farewell to you; and you; and you, Volumnius.
    Strato, thou hast been all this while asleep.
    Farewell to thee too, Strato. Countrymen,
    My heart doth joy that yet in all my life
    I found no man but he was true to me.
    I shall have glory by this losing day
    More than Octavius and Mark Antony
    By this vile conquest shall attain unto.   38
    So fare you well at once; for Brutus' tongue   39
    Hath almost ended his life's history.
    Night hangs upon mine eyes; my bones would rest,
    That have but labored to attain this hour.   42
        Alarum. Cry within: Fly, fly, fly!

CLITUS
    Fly, my lord, fly!

BRUTUS   Hence! I will follow.
        [Exeunt Clitus, Dardanius, and Volumnius.]
    I prithee, Strato, stay thou by thy lord.
    Thou art a fellow of a good respect;   45
    Thy life hath had some smatch of honor in it.   46
    Hold then my sword, and turn away thy face
    While I do run upon it. Wilt thou, Strato?

STRATO
    Give me your hand first. Fare you well, my lord.

---

38 *vile conquest* i.e. the destruction of Republican Rome   **39** *at once* all
together   **42** *but labored* experienced only pain   **45** *respect* reputation   **46**
smatch taste

BRUTUS

Farewell, good Strato. Caesar, now be still.
I killed not thee with half so good a will.
  [He runs on his sword and] dies.
  Alarum. Retreat. Enter Octavius, Antony,
  Messala, Lucilius, and the Army.

OCTAVIUS

What man is that?

MESSALA

53   My master's man. Strato, where is thy master?

STRATO

Free from the bondage you are in, Messala.

55   The conquerors can but make a fire of him;

56   For Brutus only overcame himself,
And no man else hath honor by his death.

LUCILIUS

So Brutus should be found. I thank thee, Brutus,

59   That thou hast proved Lucilius' saying true.

OCTAVIUS

60   All that served Brutus, I will entertain them.

61   Fellow, wilt thou bestow thy time with me?

STRATO

62   Ay, if Messala will prefer me to you.

OCTAVIUS

Do so, good Messala.

MESSALA

How died my master, Strato?

STRATO

I held the sword, and he did run on it.

MESSALA

66   Octavius, then take him to follow thee,

67   That did the latest service to my master.

---

53 *man* servant   55 *make a fire of* cremate   56 *Brutus only overcame* only
Brutus defeated   59 *saying* (see V, iv, 21–25)   60 *entertain them* take them
into my service   61 *Fellow* (addressed to Strato); *bestow* spend   62 *prefer*
recommend   66 *follow* serve   67 *latest* last, final

130

ANTONY

> This was the noblest Roman of them all.
> All the conspirators save only he
> Did that they did in envy of great Caesar;
> He, only in a general honest thought   71
> And common good to all, made one of them.   72
> His life was gentle, and the elements   73
> So mixed in him that Nature might stand up   74
> And say to all the world, 'This was a man!'   75

OCTAVIUS

> According to his virtue let us use him,   76
> With all respect and rites of burial.
> Within my tent his bones to-night shall lie,
> Most like a soldier, orderèd honorably.   79
> So call the field to rest, and let's away   80
> To part the glories of this happy day.   81

Exeunt omnes.

71–72 *general . . . all* honorable purpose to the whole society and for the good of all Romans   72 *made . . . them* joined the conspiracy   73 *gentle* noble; *elements* the four elements (earth, water, air, fire) of which all matter was thought to be composed, or the four humors (melancholic, phlegmatic, sanguine, choleric)   74 *So mixed* i.e. equally balanced   75 *a man* i.e. an ideal man   76 *use* treat   79 *orderèd* treated   80 *field* army   81 *part* share, divide

A selection of books published by Penguin is listed on the following pages.

For a complete list of books available from Penguin in the United States, write to Dept. DG, Penguin Books, 299 Murray Hill Parkway, East Rutherford, New Jersey 07073.

For a complete list of books available from Penguin in Canada, write to Penguin Books Canada Limited, 2801 John Street, Markham, Ontario L3R 1B4.

If you live in the British Isles, write to Dept. EP, Penguin Books Ltd, Harmondsworth, Middlesex.

THE PENGUIN ENGLISH LIBRARY

The Penguin English Library Series reproduces, in convenient but authoritative editions, many of the greatest classics in English literature from Elizabethan times through the nineteenth century. Each volume is introduced by a critical essay, enhancing the understanding and enjoyment of the work for the student and general reader alike. A few selections from the list of more than one hundred titles follow:

PERSUASION, *Jane Austen*
PRIDE AND PREJUDICE, *Jane Austen*
SENSE AND SENSIBILITY, *Jane Austen*
JANE EYRE, *Charlotte Brontë*
WUTHERING HEIGHTS, *Emily Brontë*
THE WAY OF ALL FLESH, *Samuel Butler*
THE WOMAN IN WHITE, *Wilkie Collins*
GREAT EXPECTATIONS, *Charles Dickens*
HARD TIMES, *Charles Dickens*
MIDDLEMARCH, *George Eliot*
TOM JONES, *Henry Fielding*
WIVES AND DAUGHTERS, *Elizabeth Gaskell*
MOBY DICK, *Herman Melville*
THE SCIENCE FICTION OF EDGAR ALLAN POE
VANITY FAIR, *William Makepeace Thackeray*
CAN YOU FORGIVE HER?, *Anthony Trollope*
PHINEAS FINN, *Anthony Trollope*
THE NATURAL HISTORY OF SELBORNE, *Gilbert White*

PENGUIN CLASSICS

The Penguin Classics, the earliest and most varied series of world masterpieces to be published in paperback, began in 1946 with E. V. Rieu's now famous translation of *The Odyssey*. Since then the series has commanded the unqualified respect of scholars and teachers throughout the English-speaking world. It now includes more than three hundred volumes, and the number increases yearly. In them, the great writings of all ages and civilizations are rendered into vivid, living English that captures both the spirit and the content of the original. Each volume begins with an introductory essay, and most contain notes, maps, glossaries, or other material to assist the reader in appreciating the work fully. Some volumes available include:

PLAYS BY BERNARD SHAW

ANDROCLES AND THE LION

THE APPLE CART

ARMS AND THE MAN

BACK TO METHUSELAH

CAESAR AND CLEOPATRA

CANDIDA

THE DEVIL'S DISCIPLE

THE DOCTOR'S DILEMMA

HEARTBREAK HOUSE

MAJOR BARBARA

MAN AND SUPERMAN

THE MILLIONAIRESS

PLAYS UNPLEASANT
*(Widowers' Houses, The Philanderer,
Mrs Warren's Profession)*

PYGMALION

SAINT JOAN

SELECTED ONE ACT PLAYS
*(The Shewing-up of Blanco Posnet, How He Lied to Her
Husband, O'Flaherty V.C., The Inca of Perusalem, Anna-
janska, Village Wooing, The Dark Lady of the Sonnets,
Overruled, Great Catherine, Augustus Does His Bit, The
Six of Calais)*